Lucas tore his mouth from hers.

"So much for my so-called pathetic attempts at seduction, *chica*. As for your response... very nicely done. It's everything a man could want in a woman. Sweet. Passionate. And unfortunately a little too convincing. I cannot imagine a virgin would return a kiss with such fervour."

Alyssa lunged at him, fist raised. Lucas wrapped his hand around hers.

"You can understand, then, if I inform you that your comments about seduction strike me as a tease rather than a complaint."

THE BILLIONAIRES' BRIDES

by Sandra Marton

Pregnant by their princes...

Take three incredibly wealthy European princes and
match them with three beautiful, spirited women.
Add large helpings of intense emotion
and passionate attraction. Result: three unexpected
pregnancies...and three possible princesses—
if those princes have their way…

THE ITALIAN PRINCE'S PREGNANT BRIDE
Available in June

THE GREEK PRINCE'S CHOSEN WIFE
Available in September

THE SPANISH PRINCE'S VIRGIN BRIDE
Available in December

THE
SPANISH PRINCE'S
VIRGIN BRIDE

BY
SANDRA MARTON

MILLS & BOON®
Pure reading pleasure

First published in Great Britain 2007
Harlequin Mills & Boon Limited,
Eton House, 18-24 Paradise Road, Richmond, Surrey TW9 1SR

© Sandra Marton 2007

ISBN: 978 0 263 19703 7

Set in Times Roman 10½ on 12¼ pt
07-1007-46424

Printed and bound in Great Britain
by Antony Rowe Ltd, Chippenham, Wiltshire

THE
SPANISH PRINCE'S
VIRGIN BRIDE

CHAPTER ONE

His name was Lucas Reyes.

At least, that was the name he preferred.

He was also His Highness Prince Lucas Carlos Alessandro Reyes Sanchez of Andalusia and Castile, heir to a throne that had ceased to exist centuries ago, which made him the great-great-great-*Dios,* too many "greats" to count-grandson of a king who had been among the conquistadores who tamed a distant land.

That land was America and as far as Lucas could tell, once you reached Texas you knew that those conquistadores only thought they had tamed the land.

Or so it seemed on this hot summer afternoon.

Lucas was driving his rented car along an unpaved excuse for a road beneath the glare of a merciless sun. Rain clouds hung on the distant horizon; at first, he'd foolishly thought they would bring some relief but the clouds seemed painted on an endless blue sky.

Nothing moved, except for the car, and the engine seemed to require more effort to manage even that.

Lucas tightened his hands on the steering wheel and mouthed a short, succinct oath.

He was on his way to a place called El Rancho Grande.

His grandfather had been in communication with its owner, Aloysius McDonough, who had assured them, via e-mail, this road would lead straight to it.

And pigs can fly, Lucas thought dourly.

The road was taking him nowhere except further into sagebrush and tumbleweed, and the only thing he'd seen thus far that was close to *grande* was an enormous rattlesnake.

The sight of the snake had sent Lucas's mistress into near-hysteria.

"A python," she'd screeched. "Oh God, Lucas, a python!"

He thought of pointing out that pythons didn't live in North America, then decided against it. Delia wouldn't give a damn if the creature curled by the side of the road was an alligator. It would be just one more thing to gripe about.

She'd spent most of the first hour telling him the landscape was dull and the rental car was horrible.

At least they could agree on that. One glance at a map and Lucas had told his PA to arrange for a truck or an SUV but the girl behind the rental counter insisted his PA had booked what looked to Lucas like an anchovy tin on wheels. He'd protested but it got him nowhere.

The car was all they had available.

"But we might have something else tomorrow," the girl had said brightly.

And spend more time on this fool's errand? Lucas snorted. That wasn't an option. So he'd signed for the anchovy tin, then listened to Delia whine when he said there was no room for her overnight suitcase, hanging garment bag, bulky makeup and jewelry cases in the miniscule trunk.

"We're not going to be more than a few hours at the most," he'd said impatiently.

Still, she'd protested and he'd finally told her she had

two choices. She could leave everything on his plane or she could shut up and get into the car with whatever fit.

She'd gotten into the car, but she had not shut up. She'd complained and complained about the stuff she'd had to leave behind, about the vehicle, about the road, and now she'd taken up a new refrain.

"When will we get there?"

He'd gone from saying *Soon* to *In a little while* to *We will get there when we get there,* the words delivered through gritted teeth.

"But when?" she was in the middle of saying when the anchovy tin disguised as a car groaned in fishy agony and came to a stop.

Then there was only silence.

"Lucas, why did we stop? Why did you turn off the air conditioner? When will we get there? Lucas? When—"

He swung toward Delia. Under his cool hazel glower, she sank back in her seat. Still, she couldn't resist one last comment.

"I don't know what we're doing in a place like this anyway," she said petulantly.

That was another thing they agreed on. The road, the car, and now this.

What in hell *were* they doing here?

Actually the answer was simple. Delia was here because Lucas was supposed to have taken her to the Hamptons this weekend. When he told her he couldn't, she'd pouted until he said he'd take her to Texas with him.

Lucas was here because his grandfather had suddenly told him that he was expected to meet with Aloysius McDonough at a Texas ranch called El Rancho Grande.

"Who is this man?" Lucas had asked. "I've never heard of him or his ranch."

Felix said that McDonough raised Andalusians.

"And?" Lucas asked, because surely there was more to the request than that. El Rancho Reyes raised some of the finest Andalusians in the world, surely the finest in Spain. If a pretentiously named ranch in Texas raised them, too, he'd have heard of it.

"And," Felix said, "he has something that I hope will interest you."

"A horse?" Lucas said in thinly veiled disbelief. "A stud?"

His grandfather had smiled. Actually, he'd chuckled. Lucas's eyebrows lifted.

"Have I said something amusing, Grandfather?"

"Not at all. It's just… No. Not a stud."

"You want me to look at an Andalusian mare on a ranch no one's ever heard of?"

"She's not Andalusian."

Dios, was Felix's mind starting to go? "But Andalusians are what we breed," Lucas said gently.

The old man glared at him. "Do I seem senile to you, boy? I know what we breed. I have been assured that she has excellent lineage and fine conformation."

"There are mares in Spain with those qualities."

Felix had nodded. "There are. But thus far, none has what I consider enough intelligence, beauty and heart to improve our line."

Since Lucas ran El Rancho Reyes and had been running it for a decade, he was surprised by that pronouncement.

"I didn't know you were looking, Grandfather."

"I have been looking for years, Lucas."

Another cryptic statement. The ranch had several excellent mares. In fact, Lucas had bought another one only recently…and yet, Felix sounded certain.

Lucas looked at his grandfather. *Do I look senile?* he'd said, but Felix had just passed his eighty-fifth birthday…

"Ah, Lucas, you are as transparent now as you were when you were a boy, trying to convince me to let you break your first horse." Felix chuckled and wrapped an arm around Lucas's shoulders. "I promise you, *mi hijo,* my mind is perfectly clear. You must trust me in this. I am not sending you on a wild-goose chase."

Lucas had sighed. "You really want me to go all the way to Texas for something we don't need?"

"If we did not need it, I would not ask you to go."

"I don't agree."

Felix had raised one bushy white eyebrow. "Did I ask you to agree?"

That had ended the discussion. Nobody gave Lucas Reyes orders but he loved his grandfather with all his heart. The old man had all but raised him and provided the only love Lucas had known.

So Lucas had shrugged and said, *si,* he would go to Texas even though he did not deserve such a punishment.

He'd meant it lightly but for some reason, Felix had laughed as if it were the best joke he'd ever heard.

"Lucas," he'd said, "I promise you, what awaits you in Texas is precisely what you deserve."

Now, looking at the empty road, the empty sky, the blinding sun and the woman sulking beside him, Lucas decided that his grandfather was wrong.

Nobody deserved this.

"Aren't you going to start the car?"

Delia's voice was fraught with indignation. Lucas didn't waste time answering. Instead he turned the key. Tromped on the gas pedal. Turned the key again…

Nada.

Muttering something that would have delighted the street urchins in Seville, he released the hood latch, opened the door and stepped outside.

The heat hit him like a fist even though he'd expected it.

Unlike Delia, who was decked out in a gender-challenged designer's misbegotten notion of the Old West, Lucas had dressed for the realities of a Texas summer.

Boots, of course. Not shiny and new but comfortable and well-worn. What else did a man wear when he was going to spend the day ankle-deep in horse apples? Boots and jeans, faded and washed to the softness of silk, and a pale gray chambray shirt, collar open, sleeves rolled up.

In other words, he was sensibly dressed. It didn't matter. One step from the car and he was drenched in sweat.

"Ohmygod," Delia screeched dramatically, "I'll burn up if you don't shut that door!"

Lucas obliged, slamming it with enough force that the vehicle shuddered. Jaw set, he stalked to the hood, lifted it and peered inside. Then he got down in the dirt and looked at the car's undercarriage. Neither action told him anything more than he already knew.

This sad excuse for a car was roadkill.

He dug his cell phone from his pocket, flipped it open and saw those dreaded words. *No Service.*

"*Mierda,*" he muttered and banged his fist on Delia's window. "Open the door!"

She glared and cracked it an ungracious inch. "What?"

"Do you have your cell phone?"

"Why?"

Could a man's back teeth really shatter if he ground them together too hard?

"Do you have it or not?"

A put-upon sigh before she reached into the doll-size purse that hung from her shoulder.

The purse was white leather.

Everything she wore was white leather. The ridiculous sombrero perched on her artfully-coiffed hair. The tiny fringed vest. The tight pants. The boots with four inch stiletto heels. She looked ridiculous, Lucas thought and realized, with icy certainty, that what had been dawning on him for a while was true.

Their affair had run its predictable course. As soon as they got back to New York, he'd end it.

As if she'd read his mind, Delia all but slapped the phone into his outstretched palm. A glance told him she used a different wireless provider. Maybe there was hope.

At least, when he flipped the phone open, he didn't see the ominous *No Service.*

But he couldn't get a transmission bar, either.

He held the phone at arm's length. At shoulder height. He went through the inane dance steps of the frustrated wireless user.

Nothing.

Cursing under his breath, he went to the front of the car. To the rear. Trotted up the road. Down the road. Stepped across the narrow, gravel-filled culvert that ran alongside it. Stepped back into the road. Into the middle of the road…

Miracle of miracles, a bar blinked to life on the screen.

Lucas grinned, pumped his fist in the air—and lost the bar. Easy, he told himself, easy. Move an inch at a time. Watch that screen…

Yes!

The bar was back. And another. And another…

"Look ooouut…"

His head came up. A horse the size of a brontosaurus

was galloping toward him, a rider hunched over its neck. He saw the animal's dilated nostrils, heard the pounding of its hooves…

"Damn it, look *ooouut…*"

The yell came from the rider. Lucas jumped back, stumbled and rolled into the culvert as the horse thundered past with barely an inch to spare.

Lucas shot to his feet. He shouted; the rider looked back. Lucas saw a worn ball cap. A grungy T-shirt. Jeans. Boots.

And a boy's startled face.

The rider was a kid, damn it, skinny and long-legged, riding without a saddle or stirrups. Was riding people down what passed for fun in this anteroom of hell?

Lucas shook his fist. Let fly with a string of Spanish obscenities.

The kid laughed.

Fury welled in Lucas's gut. If only the damned car worked! He'd jump into it, gun the engine, catch up to the horse. Pull the reckless brat off its back and teach him a lesson!

A gust of wind swept down from out of nowhere, plucked at the dust rising in the horse's wake. When it settled, horse and rider were gone.

"Lucas? Are you all right?"

He shot a look at the car. The near-collision had, at least, driven Delia out of it.

"I'm fine," he growled.

"That horrid animal! I thought it had killed you."

Lucas dusted off his jeans. "And you wondered," he said tersely, "how in hell you'd get out of here on your own."

"You're in a horrible mood today, Lucas. I was worried about you. Yes, perhaps I did wonder…" Delia's eyes widened. She giggled.

"You find this amusing?"

"Well, no. It's just that you have something in your hair…"

He reached up. Closed his fingers around a handful of tumbleweed and threw it aside.

"I'm delighted to be the source of your entertainment."

"Don't be such a grouch." Delia slapped her hands on her hips. "You can't blame me for—"

"No." His voice was flat as he walked toward her. "I blame only myself for our situation, Delia. Not you."

Her expression brightened. "I'm glad you understand."

Lucas reached into the car for his hat. Then he patted his thigh.

"Put your foot here."

Delia gave a breathy laugh. "Lucas," she purred, "do you really think this is the place to—"

"Your foot," he said impatiently.

Smiling, she leaned back against the door, raised one leg and put it against his thigh. He grunted, took her foot in his hands and broke off the heel of her boot.

"Hey!" Delia jerked her leg back. "What are you doing? Do you have any idea what I paid for these boots?"

"No," he said bluntly, "but I will, once I see my Amex bill this month." His eyes met hers. "Or are you going to tell me I didn't pay for that ridiculous outfit you're wearing?"

"Ridiculous? I'll have you know—"

Lucas squatted down, grabbed her other foot and snapped the heel off that boot, too.

"Now you'll be able to walk."

"Walk?" Her voice rose. "Walk where? I am not walking anywhere in this heat, on this road, with pythons and wild horses and crazy people all around… Lucas? Lucas, where are you going?"

He didn't answer. After a moment, she came trotting up alongside him.

"I hate this place," she muttered. "Never take me to Texas again!"

He would never take her anywhere again, he thought grimly. That was something else on which they could agree.

Twenty minutes and a thousand complaints later, he heard the grumble of an engine. A red pickup appeared on the horizon.

"Thank God," Delia said dramatically, and sank down on the edge of the road.

Lucas stepped into the truck's path. It was going to stop, one way or another. The hot, endless trudge to nowhere was bad enough but if he had to spend another minute listening to Delia…

The truck slowed. Stopped. The driver's door opened. A kid stepped out and Lucas felt his blood pressure rise. Was it the one who'd almost ridden him down?

It wasn't.

The rider had been slender with big dark eyes and black curls tumbling over his forehead from under his hat. This boy was redheaded and chunky.

"Howdy."

Flaking letters on the truck's door spelled out El Rancho Grande. El Rancho Bankrupto, judging by the condition of the ancient vehicle.

"Heard you folks might need a ride."

"And just who, precisely, did you hear that from?" Lucas said tightly. "A boy riding a war horse?"

The kid chuckled. "That's funny, mister."

"Everything around here is funny," Lucas said, his tone low and dangerous.

"I didn't mean it that way, I only meant—"

"For goodness' sakes," Delia said sharply, "will you

stop being so touchy, Lucas? Of course we need a ride." She shot a look at the truck. "But not in that—that thing."

The boy was looking at Delia as if he'd never seen anything like her before—which, Lucas thought grimly, he undoubtedly had not.

"Get in the truck, Delia."

Delia snorted. "I am not getting into that—"

Lucas said something ugly and hoisted her as if she were a sack of oats. She yelped as he dumped her unceremoniously on the truck's bench seat.

"In all honesty, Lucas—"

"In all honesty, Delia," he said coldly, "as soon as we reach a telephone, I'll arrange for a car to take you to the airport."

"We're going back to the city?"

"You're going," he said. "Just you."

Delia opened her mouth. So did the kid who'd climbed behind the wheel. Lucas glared at them both as he got into the truck and slammed the door.

"Just drive," he told the boy.

Delia's eyes burned with anger but she didn't argue. The kid was just as smart. He gulped, muttered, "Yessir," and hit the gas.

Two hours later, Lucas was feeling a little better.

He'd finally arrived at El Rancho Grande—and yes, the name was definitely a poor choice but he was stuck here until the rancher he'd come all this distance to see showed up. They'd had an appointment but evidently appointments were just another source of amusement in this part of Texas.

At least Delia was gone. That was something to celebrate.

He'd tried to phone for a limo or a taxi and both the boy and an old man who'd introduced himself as the ranch foreman had looked at him as if he were crazy.

"We ain't got nothin' like that here," the foreman said.

Delia had batted her lashes. "I guess you'll just have to keep me," she'd said, though her sweet tone had not matched the sly smile on her lips.

He'd sooner have kept the rattler they'd seen on the road, especially when the rental company said they couldn't get a replacement vehicle to him until the next morning.

Bad enough he'd be stuck here overnight. He sure as hell wasn't going to spend it fending off Delia.

So he'd offered the kid with the truck a sum that had made the kid's eyes bulge to retrieve her luggage from the car, then drive her to the airport. Then he'd closed his ears to what Delia wished him and watched the pickup bounce away.

The foreman had watched, too.

"Should be an interestin' trip for the lady," he'd said mildly.

"Should be interesting for both of them," Lucas had replied, and the old man had grinned.

Then Lucas had asked the million-dollar question. Where was Aloysius McDonough? He might as well have asked about Godzilla, considering the old man's wide-eyed reaction.

"You come here to see Mr. McDonough?"

No, Lucas had thought, I came for the scenery. Instead he'd smiled politely, or as politely as possible, all things considered.

"*Si.* He is expecting me."

"Do tell," the foreman had answered, spitting a thin brown stream of tobacco juice into the dry dirt. "Well, only thing I can suggest is that you hang around until this evenin'."

"McDonough will be back by then?"

The foreman shrugged. "Just wait until evenin', is what I'm sayin'. We got a guest room you can have, if you ain't particular."

"I'm sure it will be fine."

The foreman had led Lucas into the house, through rooms that were shabby but clean to one with a narrow bed and a view of the unchanging land that stretched endlessly toward the horizon.

"You want anythin', just holler."

"I'm fine," Lucas had answered. Then his eyes had narrowed. "Come to think of it… Do you have a boy working here?"

The old man shifted his wad of chewing tobacco from one side of his jaw to the other.

"Ain't you just seen Davey?"

"Not him. A different kid. One who rides a black stallion without giving a damn for anybody else."

Nope, the foreman said, he and Davey were the only hands.

Then he'd cackled like a deranged duck. Lucas could hear the sound of his laughter even after he shuffled out of the room.

Now, standing on a sagging porch, Lucas sighed. Who knew what passed for humor in a godforsaken place like this?

Besides, what did it matter? This time tomorrow, he'd be on his way home.

Assuming, he thought irritably, Aloysius McDonough showed up. Where in hell was he? Where was the supposed wonder-mare? Truth was, he doubted if there were any horses here. The corrals were empty; the out-buildings were all in bad shape. The breeze that had come up might just—

What was that?

Lucas cocked his head. He could hear a sound on the wind. A horse. Yes. A whinny. Faint, but distinct.

Maybe McDonough was back.

The sooner he saw the mare—assuming one even existed—and told a couple of polite lies about what a fine animal she was but how, unfortunately, he wasn't buying horses right now, blah blah blah...

Definitely the sooner he got this over with, the better.

Lucas stepped off the porch and started briskly toward the outbuildings. He was right about their condition. The first, a storage shed, was on the verge of collapse. The barn that came next wasn't any better.

The third building was a stable, in better shape than the other two. It needed paint and some of the boards would have benefited from a hammer and nails but when he peered in the open door, he saw the signs a horseman learns to recognize as evidence of responsible care.

The floor was clean, the two empty stalls to his left were well-swept. A stack of buckets stood beside a hose and across from stacked bales of hay.

There it was again. The soft whinny of a horse. Yes, there was an animal here.

The mare, he hoped.

Mystery solved.

Lucas hesitated. Protocol demanded a man wait to be asked onto another man's property. He frowned. To hell with protocol, which also demanded that McDonough should have been here to greet his guest.

Quietly, so he wouldn't spook the mare, he stepped inside the stable, looked past the row of empty stalls and saw a tail, a rump...

The horse danced back and Lucas's eyebrows rose.

This was not a mare. Hell, no. It was a stallion. No doubt about that, judging from the rest of what he could see.

Lucas's eyes narrowed. Not just a stallion. A black stallion.

He took a step forward. A floorboard creaked under his

weight and the stallion snorted. Metal tinkled. The animal must still be bridled and tossing its head.

"Easy," a voice said softly. "Easy, baby."

Baby? A misnomer if ever he'd heard one, but the voice was right. It was a husky voice. A boy's voice.

Lucas knotted his hands into fists and strode quickly to the stall. The horse sensed his presence before the kid standing next to it and whinnied with alarm.

Too late, Lucas thought grimly.

He'd found them. The rider and the beast that had ridden him off the road.

The kid, back to the aisle, was still oblivious, holding on to the stallion's bridle with one hand, speaking softly to the creature as he stroked its ears with the other.

"Such a charming picture," Lucas snarled, clapping his big, calloused hand over the boy's.

"Hey," the boy said indignantly.

"Hey, indeed," Lucas said with grim satisfaction, and swung the kid around.

It was him, all right. Beat-up ball cap. Grimy T-shirt. Dirty jeans, dirtier boots...

Except, when the kid's cap fell off, Lucas's jaw dropped.

The rider wasn't a boy.

She was a woman.

CHAPTER TWO

A WOMAN?

Maybe not. Maybe she was a teenaged brat. It was difficult to tell.

The rider's face was smeared with dirt, one streak angling across a sharp cheekbone, another across the bridge of her nose. Her hair, a long, heavy braid of inky-black, fell over her shoulder and across her breast.

Lucas's gaze followed the path of that braid...and knew she was most definitely a grown woman.

Her T-shirt was sweat-soaked. It clung to her body, the cotton wet and all but translucent as it molded her rounded breasts and taut nipples.

Lucas's body reacted, enraging him even more. To be damned near ridden down, then laughed at by an adult female, and now to have an atavistic reaction to that female...

He heard the harsh rasp of her indrawn breath. Instantly he cupped her jaw and silenced her scream before it started.

"Do not," he said grimly, "do anything you'll regret."

She stared at him through wild eyes. He let it go on for a long moment, relishing every instant before he finally spoke.

"Don't tell me you don't recognize me, *amada*." He

smiled thinly. "I'd hate to think our meeting was not as memorable for you as it was for me."

Something flashed in the depths of those amazingly blue eyes. She remembered him, all right.

Except, this time he was the one laughing, she was the one in danger. And she knew it. What he'd seen in her eyes was fear.

Good. A woman might well show fear when confronted by a man her horse had almost trampled.

The big stallion snorted and shifted his formidable weight with surprising delicacy on hooves the size of dessert plates. Lucas moved his grasp to the woman's arm and dragged her toward him.

She didn't make it easy. Her lean, feminine body was surprisingly well-muscled, especially when she dug in her boot heels, but she was no match for him. Not in size or weight or tight-lipped anger. A couple of seconds and he had her trapped between him and the wall.

"It was an accident."

"Ah. You do remember me after all."

"You were standing in the middle of the road—"

"Is standing in the road against the law in Texas?"

She was trying to control her fear or, at least, trying to mask it. And she was doing a fairly good job. The steadiness in her voice might have fooled him if he hadn't seen the race of her pulse in the hollow of her throat.

"Trespassing on private property is."

"That road isn't private property. Besides, whatever happened to southwestern hospitality? I'm visiting. Surely that's permitted in Texas."

"All right. You made your point. Now do yourself a favor and go away before I—"

"Before you what?" Lucas jerked his head toward the

stallion. "Before you get on the back of that beast and try to run me down again?"

"I did not try to run you down," she said coldly. "If I had, you wouldn't be here making an ass of yourself."

"Such bravado," he said softly.

"What do you want?"

"Why, what could I possibly want?" He reached out, ran a lazy hand down her throat; she jerked like a skittish mare under his touch. "Just a little chat."

That put the balance of power back where it belonged. Fear blossomed in her eyes again.

"If you think I'm alone here—"

"Of course you're not alone." His voice was deliberately soft, his tone just this side of condescending. "There's an old man up at the house who could surely help you—if he were thirty years younger. And there's a boy. Well, there *was* a boy."

Her face paled. "What have you done with Davey?"

Lucas gave a negligent shrug. "I took care of him."

Her pupils widened, the darkness all but swallowing the blue fire of her eyes.

"Tell me what you've done with Davey."

"Davey's welfare is not your problem."

Her chin lifted. She was defiant, despite her fear. He had to give her grudging credit for that.

"I sent him on an errand."

"To where?"

"Damn it," he growled, "the boy is fine! I'm not interested in discussing him." He tightened his grasp on her wrist. "I'm talking about you, *señorita*. You could have killed me."

"But I didn't. That's what matters. Bebé and I didn't harm a hair on your head."

"Bebé," he scoffed. "A charming name for a behemoth."

"If you hadn't been standing in the middle of the road—"

"If you'd been in control of that monster—"

"Standing in the middle of the road, fooling around with a gadget anyone with half a brain would know couldn't possibly work out here—"

"Nothing works out here," Lucas snapped, "not even human courtesy. I was not, as you so generously put it, 'fooling around' with my phone. My car broke down, or didn't you notice it by the side of the road?"

"Of course I noticed! I sent Davey back to get you." Her eyebrows lifted. "Is that what you call that silly excuse for transportation?" she said sweetly. "A car?"

"Please," Lucas said coldly, "don't hold back. There's no need to watch what you say on my account."

"Well, you set yourself up for it, didn't you? Expecting a mobile phone to work out here, driving a thing like that on back roads…"

Dios, this was the stupidest quarrel he'd had since he was eight and in a nose-to-nose battle over whether *Real Madrid* or *Futbol Club Barcelona* fielded the better soccer team.

What was wrong with this woman? Arguing with him, angering him when for all she knew, he was a madman come to do her harm. And when in hell, *how* in hell, had she managed to turn the tables?

He was the injured party here, not she.

"Anyway," she said, "this is all beside the point. I didn't hurt you. Except…well, maybe your pride. I mean, we both know you ended up in a ditch…"

Lucas saw her lips twitch. Could a man's blood pressure rise to the point where he exploded?

"And," he said silkily, "you found it amusing."

"No," she said, but there was that twitch again.

"You know," he said softly, "a smart woman might consider a simple apology appropriate just about now."

That gave her pause. He could almost see her weighing her options. She was alone with a stranger, nobody to turn to for help.

On the other hand, he had a strong suspicion the word "apology" was not a normal part of her vocabulary.

A long moment passed. Then she huffed out a breath that lifted the silky, jet-black curls from her forehead.

"Yes. Okay. I shouldn't have laughed."

"Or tried to run me down."

"I told you, I did not try to run you down." She hesitated. "But I guess it was impolite to find the situation amusing."

"The understatement of the century."

"It's just that…it was—it was interesting. You, dressed as if you might actually know one end of a horse from another—"

"Which," he said coldly, "is surely an impossibility."

"And your lady friend… Was that get-up left over from Halloween or what?"

If this was her idea of an apology, he could only imagine what she would consider an insult.

"My lady friend," he said, lying through his teeth in a last desperate attempt at maintaining the upper hand, "was simply wearing what any attractive woman would wear."

"To a masquerade party, maybe."

She was right, but he'd be damned if he'd let her know it.

"To ride a horse in Central Park," Lucas said, lying again and fervently hoping all the horses who called Manhattan home would forgive him. He took a step back, his hand still wrapped around her wrist, and gave her a long, slow look. "But then, what would you know about being a woman in a place like New York?" He took another long, lazy look at her, from her toes to the top of her head. "You are a woman, aren't you, *amada?* Under all that ridiculous clothing?"

Dios, he thought, hearing himself, picturing himself, what was he doing? The leer, the line—it was all such bull.

And yet, to his surprise, it had its effect.

The rider blinked. One blink, that was all, but enough to tell him she'd suddenly remembered she was in a situation she didn't control.

"Okay." Her tone was cool but, yes, there was an underlying tremor. "I've apologized. Now you can let go of my wrist, say *adios* and get out of here."

"Tomorrow," Lucas said softly.

"Tomorrow, what?"

"I'll leave tomorrow, when the rental agency sends a replacement for my car."

"You are not spending the night on this ranch!"

"Somehow, I doubt that is your decision to make."

The stallion snorted and stamped a powerful hoof.

"Bebé's upset," the woman said.

"So am I."

"He can be dangerous, especially if he thinks I need protection."

"I assure you, *amada,* I can be far more dangerous than the horse."

He let the softly spoken words hang in the air, watching with grim satisfaction as they had their desired effect.

At last, she took a deep breath.

"Whatever you're thinking—"

"I suspect I'm thinking the same thing you are," Lucas said with a thin smile.

He could almost see her in frantic debate with herself. Part of her wanted to spit in his eye but another part—the wiser part—was reminding her that this was not a good situation.

"Look," she finally said, "I didn't try to ride you down on purpose. Bebé is fast. And I was bent over his head, talking to him—"

"What?"

"He's high-strung. Listening to me soothes him. Horses respond to a person's voice."

"They respond better to riders who can control them."

"What could you possibly know about horses?"

Lucas grinned. "Perhaps a little something."

"Really?" She stood glaring at him, one booted foot tapping the wide-boarded floor, and he knew the wiser part of her had lost the argument. "For instance? What 'little something' do you know?"

"I know that this so-called ranch is on its last legs."

Color swept into her face. "Really."

"I know that you have no stock, aside from that creature you call Bebé."

Her chin jerked up. "So?"

"So," Lucas said coldly, "that is the reason I was asked to come here."

Her eyes widened. "What do you mean, you were asked to come here? By whom?"

"By the owner. I was told there was a mare for sale."

"A mare?"

"*Si*. Breeding stock for me."

She was looking at him as if he'd lost his mind. For once, he could hardly blame her.

"For my stallions," he amended. "My Andalusians. *Pura Raza Espanola.*" Lucas's gaze hardened. "But there is no mare here. No PRE stock at all—not even that ugly thing you call a stallion. Or would you like to pretend I am wrong about that, too?"

The woman wet her lips with a quick sweep of her tongue. He found himself following the simple action with hungry concentration, though why he would was beyond him.

She had spirit and fire but she was not the kind of woman who would ever interest him.

He'd seen females like her all his life. They hung around ranches. Around horse shows. Their passion was horses. They dressed like men, rode like men. As far as Lucas was concerned, they might as well have been men.

He knew exactly how he liked his women.

Sweet-smelling, with perfume in their hair, not hay. Smiling and soft-spoken, not glowering and acid-tongued. He liked to see them use feminine wiles, not pseudomasculine bravado.

He supposed some might think this woman had a pretty face, if you overlooked the smudges and smears. And, yes, her hair was an extraordinary shade of black, the color of a raven's wing. He suspected it would be heavy as raw silk, if she ever let it out of that unflattering braid and brushed it into smooth, shiny waves.

He could even admit that the rest of her had promise, too. The high, full breasts. The slender waist and curved hips. The long, long legs that could draw a man deep inside her heat...

"Who are you?"

Her voice pulled him back to reality. "What?"

"I said, what's your name?"

The tone of command was back. It made him angry enough to draw himself up to his full six foot two and respond with the icy hauteur of a man who was never questioned.

"I am Lucas Reyes."

To his surprise, her face turned white. She had heard of him, then. He found himself taking some satisfaction in that.

"No! You can't be!"

"I assure you, *señorita,* I am."

"Lucas Reyes? Prince Lucas Reyes? Of the Reyes Ranch in Spain?"

Was his hot-tempered hoyden going to throw herself at his feet? Women sometimes did, if not literally.

For some insane reason, the possibility that she would turn out to be such a woman made him even angrier, angry enough to respond with disdain.

"Not *of* the Reyes Ranch," he said, lifting his hand from her wrist. "To all intents and purposes, I *am* the Reyes Ranch."

The woman shook her head. "You're not supposed to be here."

"Really?" he purred, folding his arms.

"I sent a letter—"

"*You* sent a letter?"

"I mean—I mailed a letter. To Prince Felix Reyes. Your father."

"My grandfather. And what did this letter say?"

"It—it told you not to come."

"If there was a letter," Lucas said sharply, "neither my grandfather nor I ever saw it." He flashed a cold smile. "So, I am here, as planned. Perhaps we can agree that it is even possible I might—what was your charming phrase? I might know one end of a horse from the other."

The woman drew herself up. "Your visit is pointless. You'll have to leave."

"Are you giving me orders, *señorita?*"

"Just go, that's all."

His gaze swept over her. "What do you do here? Are you the cook? The maid? Do you muck out the stalls?"

"I do all those things."

His mouth twisted. "And warm McDonough's bed as well?"

Her hand was a blur in the rapidly fading light. Lucas caught it before she could slap him and twisted it behind her, forced her to her toes. She looked up at him through eyes gone so dark they were almost black.

"What's the matter, *amada?* Did I strike too close to home?"

"You can't talk to me that way! Not in America, you can't. We don't give a damn for stupid titles. For princes who've never sweated for a day's wages. For—for men who wouldn't know how to be men if their lives depended on it."

"Watch yourself," he said quietly.

He could almost see her struggling between defiance and caution. He knew which she'd choose before she did.

"Or you'll do what, almighty prince? Subject me to the *bastinado?*"

Maybe it was the flippant tone. The insulting words. The mention of an ancient punishment.

Or maybe it was her easy dismissal of him as a man, a dismissal made by a woman who knew nothing about being a woman.

"Why would I do that," he growled, "when there are much better things to do with a woman?"

He pulled her into his arms and kissed her. Kissed that sullen, angry mouth.

She fought him. Hands, teeth, the attempted thrust of a knee. She fought hard but Lucas threaded his hands into her hair, tipped back her head and kissed her again, harder this time, parting her lips with his so that she had no choice but to accept the swift thrust of his tongue.

Her hands came up between them, palms slapping against his shoulders, thumbs scrabbling for his eyes. He shifted his weight, pushed her back against the stable partition and went on kissing her.

She tasted of heat.

Of rage.

Of the untamed land she rode.

And, impossibly, of wildflowers that would come to life from barren soil after a summer rain.

She smelled of them, too. Not of horse, as he'd expected, or leather, but of flowers. Sweet. Exciting. And yet, somehow, tender and innocent as well.

Even struggling against him, she was soft in his arms. Incredibly soft.

Her mouth, her skin were like silk. The feel of her breasts against his chest. Her belly against his...

He swept one hand down the long length of her back. Stroked her as he would a mare afraid of a stallion's possession. Drew her toward him. Against him. Softened the pressure of his mouth on hers.

And heard the choked cry of her surrender.

She rose toward him. Her hands slid up his chest. "Don't," she whispered, but her mouth, that sweet mouth, was opening to his.

"Béseme," Lucas said thickly. "Kiss me, *amada.* Like that. Yes. Just like—"

The stable door banged open. The woman stiffened in his arms.

"Hello? Somebody in here?"

It was the foreman. Lucas tried to draw the woman deeper into the shadows but she shook her head, made a whimper of distress against his lips.

"Don't listen," Lucas whispered. "Don't answer."

"Hey!" The faint scuff of boots, then the foreman called out again. "Who's there?"

Her hands came up, slammed against Lucas's chest. "Let go," she whispered.

"That isn't what you wanted a minute ago."

"It was. Of course it—"

Lucas kissed her again. Her mouth softened, clung to his for a second before her sharp little teeth sank into his bottom lip.

He thrust her from him, dug in his pocket for a handkerchief that he pressed to his mouth. He looked at the scarlet drops of blood that stained the fine white linen, then at her.

"Reckless with men as well as with horses," he said coldly. "Dangerous behavior for a woman, *amada.*"

Her eyes blazed into his. "You were right when you said there was nothing you would want here. Do yourself a favor, Your Highness. Go back to a world you understand."

"With pleasure—as soon as I've met with your employer."

"That's not going to happen."

"Whatever I wish to happen will happen," Lucas said harshly. "The sooner you get that through your head, the better."

He thought she was going to answer but maybe she'd finally figured out that arguing with him was pointless because, instead, she dug a key from her pocket and flipped it at him.

"There's a station wagon parked in back. It's old and it's not all gussied up so you won't like it very much, but it'll get you to Dallas."

Lucas let the key fall at his feet.

"Shall I tell you what *you* need, *señorita?* Better still, shall I show you?"

"Okay," the foreman growled. "Whoever's in here, you better show yourself."

The woman's eyes blazed into Lucas's one last time. Then she swiveled on her heel and walked away.

"George," he heard her say brightly, "why don't we go to the office and look at that catalog you mentioned yesterday?"

Her voice faded. Lucas's anger didn't.

Did she really think he would tuck his tail between his legs and run? It would have taken a Texas twister to move him now.

He had come here to meet with Aloysius McDonough and that was what he would do. He owed that to his grandfather.

As for what he owed the woman… A muscle bunched in his jaw.

He would deal with her, too.

She didn't know how to handle a horse or a potential client, if there had actually been a mare worth buying in this desolate place.

She sure as hell didn't know how to handle a man.

Perhaps McDonough liked being toyed with. Lucas didn't.

McDonough needed to know what had happened here today. The woman's incompetence. Her rudeness.

Her provocative sexual games.

Lucas strode from the stable.

If anyone was going to be ordered off this sorry bit of real estate, it sure as hell would not be him.

CHAPTER THREE

BY LATE afternoon, the clouds that had hung over the horizon most of the day finally began moving.

Better still, as far as Lucas was concerned, they were building, turning into impressive thunderheads as they drew closer. Unless he was reading the signs wrong, the oppressive heat that held the valley in an iron grasp was about to break.

He threw open the guest room window in hopes of catching a breeze. There was none but the scent of rain was definitely in the air.

It couldn't come soon enough.

The guest room was boxy and hot. An ancient electric fan stood on an oak dresser but there was no way to coax more than a flutter from it. Under normal circumstances, he'd have been out the door hours ago but these were not normal circumstances.

He was as good as trapped here, thanks to a promise he'd foolishly made to his grandfather.

At least he hadn't seen the woman again. He'd gone straight through the front door, up the stairs to this room without seeing a soul. As far as he could tell, he was alone in the house.

Just where in hell was Aloysius McDonough?

Lucas looked impatiently at his watch. Five-thirty. If McDonough didn't show up soon…

If he didn't, what?

No matter what happened, he was stuck here until tomorrow, when the car rental agency delivered a replacement vehicle.

Maybe it hadn't been so smart to ignore the car key the woman had tossed him in the stable. Maybe he should go back and search for it.

Or maybe he should search for her.

Lucas snorted. He wouldn't do, either. He'd wait this out, go home and tell his grandfather that McDonough had been too ashamed to show up and admit there was no mare for sale.

Thunder rumbled in the distance and a spiked streak of lightning sizzled from the almost-black sky. The storm was coming on quickly now, turning day into night.

Hard to believe that only yesterday he'd been in Manhattan at about this same hour, having drinks with his two oldest friends, Nicolo and Damian. Drinks, some laughter…and then dinner.

Lucas's belly growled.

He hadn't eaten since early morning. There seemed to be an entirely different meaning to hospitality on El Rancho Grande. First, you damn near rode a man down, then you didn't show up for an appointment and if neither of those things got rid of an apparently unwanted guest, you tried starving him out.

Lucas folded his arms and glowered at his reflection in the age-speckled mirror over the dresser.

The possibility of that key still lying on the stable floor was growing more and more appealing. Why, when you came down to it, should he feel obligated to stay here? Hell, he'd kept *his* promise to come to this—this alien outpost.

It was Aloysius McDonough who hadn't kept his.

Was that enough reason to disappoint Felix? Lucas sighed at the obvious answer and began to pace.

He had to calm down. Otherwise, by the time McDonough deigned to show up—assuming that ever happened—he'd say or do something rash. And he didn't want that.

Who was he kidding?

He wanted exactly that. More to the point, he wanted to tell McDonough what a fool he was to run a ranch straight into the ground, to employ a woman who dressed like a man, had the surliness of a man...

And could turn hot and female despite all of that.

Was it an act? The way she'd responded when he'd kissed her? She'd inferred that it was, but Lucas was not a fool.

Women could give award-winning performances at the drop of a hat.

They could weep, if they thought tears could get them what they wanted. They could smile, if they believed that was the better choice. They could pretend that whatever interested you interested them, that they wanted nothing but you, not your title or your wealth or your power.

Oh, yes.

He knew all that and more. A man couldn't reach the age of thirty-two, couldn't have the wealth he had been born to, the even greater wealth he'd accumulated by expanding the Reyes empire, without meeting more than his share of women who were experts at plotting and planning and lying.

A thin smile crossed his mouth.

The one thing they couldn't lie about was sex.

Not that an occasional woman didn't try.

"Ohhh, Lucas," one had whispered the first time they'd made love.

The moans, the whispers, had all sounded right, but she'd been faking it. He'd known it instantly.

A woman's eyes blurred with desire when what she felt was real. Her pulse increased with the heavy beat of her blood. She trembled like a willow in her lover's arms.

The woman in his bed that time had been lying, but that hadn't angered him.

It had challenged him.

Slowly, deliberately, he'd set out to turn that carefully spoken "ohhh" into a whisper of true passion, and he had done it.

Of course he had.

He knew what tender female flesh begged for a man's touch, what hidden place would heat under a man's lips.

Without question, he knew that the woman he'd kissed a couple of hours ago had not been acting. Like it or not, she'd been as turned on by that kiss as he'd been.

Lucas frowned.

As he was now.

Dios, he truly was in desperate shape! He needed a drink, a meal, an evening back in the real world. That the memory of a woman who'd done nothing but provoke him should have such an effect on him was ridiculous.

Perhaps he'd been too hasty, sending Delia away. An hour with her in the old-fashioned bed in this room and—

And what?

Who was he kidding?

An hour with Delia, with any of the women who'd passed through his life, and he'd still want the woman from the stable in his arms, her mouth opened to the thrust of his tongue, her breasts naked and hot against his chest.

There'd been something about the feel of her skin, the shock of her surrender…

Hell.

Aloysius McDonough could take this excuse of a ranch, this forgotten appointment and stuff them. It was one thing to pay a visit out of respect for Felix but another to be made a fool of.

Lucas strode to the door, flung it open—and found the laconic foreman just about to knock.

"There you are, mister."

"But not for long," Lucas said flatly. "I'm done waiting."

"That's what I come to tell you. You don't have to wait no more."

"Damned right, I don't. A while ago, the woman who works here—"

"Ain't no woman works here."

For some reason, the confirmation of what Lucas had already figured made him even angrier.

"Your boss's woman, then," he snapped. "She gave me the key to an old car she said was parked behind the stable but I didn't…" Why was he explaining himself? "I want that key now."

"You just said—"

"I know what I said," Lucas growled. "Surely there's a second key. I want it."

"I come to tell you what I been told to tell you. You can come on down to Mr. McDonough's office now."

"You mean, he's finally here?"

But he was talking to himself. The foreman was already shuffling down the hall.

He was half-tempted to go after the man, grab him by the collar and pin him against the wall—which only proved how out of control he'd let things get.

Instead he took a steadying breath.

What was that American saying about killing two birds with one stone? He could see McDonough, then demand the damned key to the damned car and say goodbye to this damned place.

He could hardly wait.

The office was tucked behind what Lucas assumed would be known as the front parlor in a house the age of this. It was a big room furnished in oak and leather, but what caught his attention were the prints and photographs framed and hung on the walls.

Horses. Colts. Paddocks and barns and stables. It took a minute to realize the pictures were of the ranch as it must have once been. Handsome, well-tended and prosperous.

McDonough had lied about the mare he claimed to have for sale. He'd somehow let this place tumble into ruin. But he had once run it properly and understood what it meant to be a horseman.

"Depressing as all get-out, isn't it? Kind of a sad chronicle of what used to be, could have been…well, you get my drift."

Lucas swung around. A man stood in the doorway, mouth curved in a smile that could only be categorized as nervous.

He damned well should have been nervous, Lucas thought coldly, taking in the figure of his host.

Aloysius McDonough was not at all what he'd expected.

He'd envisioned a tall man, whipcord thin and weather-hardened, wearing a dark suit, bolo tie and polished boots, maybe even a Stetson.

Obviously, he thought wryly, he'd seen one too many Hollywood Westerns on late-night TV during his days at Yale.

McDonough was short and pear-shaped, dressed in a pale gray suit and shiny wing-tips. His hair was arranged in an elaborate comb-over that emphasized his balding scalp. His face was florid and damp with sweat.

Lucas disliked him on sight.

And thought, immediately, of the obscenity of the black-haired rider warming the man's bed.

Everything inside him tensed, so much so that when McDonough held out his hand, he could only stare at it. The man's wary smile dipped and Lucas took a breath and forced himself to accept the extended hand, which was as soft and clammy as he'd known it would be.

"It's a pleasure to meet you, Your Majesty."

"Please," Lucas said, smiling thinly. "I'm hardly anyone's majesty."

He withdrew his hand, fought back the desire to wipe it on his jeans. He had gotten this far; he'd see the meeting through but to hell with being polite.

Nobody had been polite to him.

The best he could offer, in honor of his grandfather's name, was to be direct.

"Mr. McDonough—"

"Please. Before we start, let me apologize Your— Your Highness. Is that correct? Is it the way to address you, I mean?"

"Just call me Reyes."

"I'm sorry for the delay, Mr. Reyes."

"Yes. So am I. We were supposed to meet hours ago."

"I know. It's just… May I get you something to drink, Prince?"

"The name is Reyes."

"Sorry. Of course. I'm not accustomed to meeting with— Well, then. What will it be? Something to eat, perhaps?"

Lucas had lost his appetite.

"Nothing, thank you. Let's just get down to business, Mr. McDonough. That's why I'm here."

McDonough's face grew shinier. "I can see that you're annoyed, Your Lordship."

Lucas thought of correcting him again but changed his mind. He had little patience for phonies and fools and from what he'd observed thus far, McDonough was both. The man could genuflect, for all he gave a damn.

"I apologize, sir. I'm sorry I wasn't here when you arrived."

"So am I."

"I assure you, it was unavoidable. I am no happier about it than you are."

McDonough wasn't kneeling but he sure as hell was shaking in his shoes. Lucas gave an inward sigh, counted silently to ten and then forced what he hoped was a convincing smile.

"Things happen," he said. "As a businessman, as a rancher, I understand that. So..." He cleared his throat. "So, let's begin again, yes? I'm pleased to meet you, Mr. McDonough. My grandfather sends warm greetings."

"Thank you, Your Highness. But—but I must tell you, I am not Aloysius McDonough."

Lucas's attempted smile failed. "Then who are you?"

"My name is Thaddeus Norton. I'm an attorney."

So much for new beginnings.

"Mr. Norton," Lucas said brusquely, "this is a waste of time. I came here to meet with Aloysius McDonough. Where is he?"

"I'll explain everything, sir, if you'll just be patient."

"I'm tired of being patient. Where is McDonough? And where is the mare?"

The attorney's face was a study in confusion. "What mare, Your Excellency?"

"The nonexistent paragon of horseflesh I came to buy."

"But—but there is no mare, sir."

"Didn't I just say that?" Lucas replied. *Dios,* now he was playing straight man in a bad comedy act. "Let me clarify things, Norton. My grandfather said he had contracted to purchase a mare. You and I both know there is no mare, so either he made a mistake or your client misrepresented the situation." Lucas's eyes narrowed. "I must tell you, my grandfather is not in the habit of making mistakes."

Norton swallowed audibly. "I don't know how to explain it, sir, but you're right, there is no mare." His Adam's apple bobbed up and down as he swallowed again. "But there is all the rest. The land. The buildings. I know things are in some disrepair but—"

And, with those words, it began to fall into place.

Felix had been duped.

McDonough didn't hope to sell a mare that would infuse the Reyes bloodlines with new intelligence, beauty and heart, he hoped to get rid of a failing property by unloading it on an old friend.

Lucas struggled to keep calm when what he wanted to do was cross the room, grab the lawyer by the collar and shake him.

"You and McDonough insult me and my grandfather," he said through his teeth. "Did you actually think I would come here to see a mare and, instead, agree to buy this— this run-down corner of purgatory?"

"Please, Your Lordship. I beg you to compose yourself."

"I am composed," Lucas roared. "I am perfectly composed! Now get Aloysius McDonough in here so I can tell him what I think of him to his face!"

"I'm afraid that's impossible."

Lucas knotted his hands into fists. It was either that or plow them into the soft gut of the man in front of him.

"So is continuing this discussion," he snarled, and strode toward the door.

"Prince Lucas! You don't understand. Aloysius McDonough is dead."

Lucas turned and stared at Thaddeus Norton. "He can't be dead. My grandfather spoke to him last week, when they agreed to this appointment."

"You must have that wrong. Aloysius passed away almost six months ago."

"I have it right, Norton. I was with my grandfather when he made the phone call."

Lucas had an excellent grasp of the English language. Still, some idioms had always eluded him. One was the phrase, "sweating bullets." He'd never understood it until now as big drops of sweat popped out on Norton's brow.

"I, ah, I don't suppose you know the exact date of that call, sir?"

It was an easy question to answer. Lucas met with Felix on Mondays. It was a courtesy to keep his grandfather up-to-date about the Reyes Corporation and its holdings.

"Last Monday, in late afternoon. It would have been morning here."

The attorney swallowed hard. "That call would have been between your grandfather and me, sir."

"*You* spoke with Felix?"

"Yes, sir."

Lucas's eyes narrowed. "Are you suggesting my grand-father sent me here, knowing McDonough was dead? That he lied to me?"

"No," Norton said quickly. "I'm sure he didn't. I—I suspect he—he just left out a couple of facts."

"A polite way of saying yes, you are suggesting my grandfather lied," Lucas said in a soft voice many had learned to fear.

"Sir. Please understand, I am only representing my client. As for my conversation with your grandfather..." Norton swallowed. "He said it was time to implement the plan he and my client agreed upon a year ago."

"What plan?"

Norton twisted his hands together. "I just assumed—I assumed your grandfather and you discussed it. That you knew—"

"Damn it, get to it! What plan?"

"Well—well, a year ago, Aloysius and your grandfather talked. About El Rancho Grande. And—"

"And," Lucas growled, "your client saw a chance to presume upon an old friendship."

"No, sir! That isn't what happened."

A muscle jumped in Lucas's jaw. The details didn't matter. McDonough had been desperate for money and he'd come up with a scheme designed to scam an old friend. Dead or not, the man was a lying, deceitful son of a bitch.

Still, why had Felix lied about the mare? About McDonough? If his grandfather knew there was no horse, knew that McDonough was dead...

Lucas would have trusted Felix with his life. To learn that trust might be misplaced...

Was Felix—was he becoming senile?

It was a terrible thought but a plausible explanation. Either Felix had lied to him or his mind was slipping. Neither prospect was good.

Lucas drew a heavy breath.

"Mr. Norton. There has been—there has been some confusion here. I can see that this has nothing to do with you."

Norton nodded in relief. "Thank you, sir."

"Obviously this matter is—it is ended." Lucas's voice grew brisk. "I assume you came here by car. I would be grateful if you would drive me to town. I have no vehicle. It's a long story and not very interesting, but—"

"Nothing is ended, Your Highness," Norton said quickly.

Lucas stiffened. "I assure you," he said coldly, "it is."

"The agreement between your grandfather and my client—"

"Damn it, man, I'm not stupid. Your client did what he could to drag my grandfather—to drag the Reyes Ranch—into his financial mess. I promise you, that's not going to happen."

Norton's Adam's apple danced again. "It's already happened, sir. Your grandfather bought El Rancho Grande a year ago. It was to change ownership upon my client's death."

Lucas was stunned. Reyes Corporation—damn it, *he* owned this disaster area?

"Last week, your grandfather phoned to say he was ready to execute the terms of the sale. That he was sending you to, uh, to implement the final contract stipulation."

"Let me see the contract."

The attorney took a large white handkerchief from his pocket and mopped his face.

"Perhaps we should discuss the stipulation first, sir, and then…"

"Damn it, Thaddeus! Stop weaseling and get to it!"

The voice, female and curt, sliced through the room. Lucas turned and stared at the woman in the doorway.

She was tall. Slender. Her midnight-black hair was drawn back in a severe knot; pearls glittered demurely at her ears and throat. In a white silk blouse, black trousers, butterscotch leather blazer and polished black riding boots, she looked like she'd just stepped out of an expensive Manhattan town house, not a stable.

And yet, that was the last place he had seen her.

His eyes narrowed. "You clean up well for a woman who earns her living mucking stalls."

The look she gave him lowered the room's temperature.

"You should have taken my advice and left El Rancho Grande, Mr. Reyes."

"And not enjoy whatever interesting little performance is about to take place?" Lucas smiled thinly. "Not on a bet."

She dug in her pocket, held out the same key she'd offered him before.

"It's not too late."

"Trust me, it is." Another thin, unpleasant smile curved his mouth. "Things are just getting interesting."

"Interesting," she said, and gave a brittle laugh.

It reminded him of how she'd laughed when she'd almost ridden him down.

"Laughter," he said carefully, "seems an inappropriate response."

"Believe me, mister, any other response is out of the question."

"Try an apology instead." He took a step toward her. "You still owe me one."

That made her laugh again. It made his blood pressure soar. He was in a game but he didn't know the rules, didn't know his opponent, didn't know the prize he was playing for.

The only certainty was that the woman was knee-deep in whatever was going on.

"You have one minute to explain," he said, moving slowly

toward her. "You or Norton. I don't give a damn who tells me what this is all about. One minute. Then I'm leaving."

"Has anyone ever told you what a pompous ass you are?"

Dios, he could feel the rage building inside him. "I warn you, *amada,* watch how you speak to me."

"The days of royalty are over, Mr. Reyes. Playing emperor won't get you anywhere. Not here. This is my country, my land, my—"

It was as if she'd pushed some hidden switch. Nothing mattered but dealing with her interminable insolence and Lucas knew exactly how to do it.

He pulled her into his arms and kissed her.

CHAPTER FOUR

HOURS ago, she'd struggled against him, then given herself up to his kiss.

Not this time.

She didn't just struggle, she fought like a wildcat. Tried to bite him. Knee him. Shove him away.

Lucas wouldn't let any of that happen.

He used his anger, his height, his leanly muscled strength to propel her back against the wall. Then he used his hands to manacle hers and pin them uselessly beside her.

Dimly he heard the attorney saying his name but he ignored that, ignored everything but the need to get even. To win. To let her know, without question, she could not laugh at him or look at him as if he were a creature worthy of her contempt.

Even in the fever that gripped him, Lucas had to admit that there was more.

There was the taste of her. Wild. Honeyed. Passionate.

The heat that rose from her silken skin.

The texture of her mouth as he invaded it.

As she fought, as he forced her to accept his kiss, the part of his brain that still clung to civility asked him what the hell he was doing.

He had never forced sexual compliance from a woman in his life.

But he wanted that from her.

No. Not compliance. Hell, never compliance.

He wanted to hear her sigh with desire. To melt under the stroke of his hands. To return his kisses and ask for more.

His mouth softened on hers. His hands lessened their grip on her wrists. He whispered to her in Spanish, words a man might use to tell his lover he would show her fulfillment beyond any she'd ever imagined...

The woman caught her breath. And became warm and pliant in his arms.

He felt the change. The delicate swell of her breasts against his chest. The almost imperceptible tilt of her hips to his. She was surrendering. Admitting that he was in command, not she.

He could let her go now...

Unless he kissed her until she begged him never to stop. Until what had started hours ago ended with his hands under her skirt, her panties torn aside so he could enter her. Thrust deep between her eagerly parted thighs as she urged him to take her, to possess her, again and again and again...

She cried out. Wrenched her hands free or perhaps he let go. Either way, Lucas stumbled back. She swayed; her eyes flew open, dark and hot with hatred.

Or with something that made him want to reach for her again.

He shuddered.

Was he insane? Was she? All he knew was that the sooner he left this place, the better.

The woman was trembling. The attorney was goggle-eyed. Lucas forced himself to speak as calmly as if nothing had happened.

"Now," he said, "perhaps we can get to the truth."

"The truth," she said, "is that you're a son of a—"

"Alyssa!" The attorney came to life and stepped quickly between them. "I suggest you not say anything you'll regret."

"Excellent advice, *amada.*"

"I have some advice for *you,* Mr. Reyes," she said in a low voice. "Get the hell out of my house!"

"Your house? Have I misunderstood something?" Lucas looked at Norton and smiled slyly. "Did your client leave the opulent El Rancho Grande to—what is it you call the lady? Alyssa?" He folded his arms. "Alyssa the what? The maid? The cook? The stable girl? My understanding—and perhaps I have it wrong—was that I own this place now." His voice hardened. "All of it, from the dried-out pastures to the collapsing barn. Is that not so, Norton?"

The lawyer looked as if he'd have given anything to disappear as he ran a shaking finger around the inside of his collar.

"That is correct, sir. Though I'm afraid—I'm afraid it's a bit more complicated than that."

"More complicated?" Lucas snorted. "My grandfather was tricked into buying a useless ranch, I was tricked into coming here and you tell me there is still more? Are you about to tell me I must rescue a captive princess from the dragon-guarded tower in which she is chained?"

Norton made a sound as if he were gagging. The woman—Alyssa—gave a bitter laugh.

"Do not laugh at me again." Lucas rounded on her, his face white with fury. "Or, I promise, you will regret it."

"What I regret," she snapped, "is that I didn't let Bebé run you into the ground!"

"Such charm," Lucas said slyly. "I trust you showed a warmer side to your lover."

"To her…?" The attorney blanched. "Sir. Let me explain who Alyssa—who this lady is."

"I've already figured that out. The only explanation I want now is what in hell you mean by this thing you call a 'stipulation.' Do I own this ranch or not?"

"Well—"

"Of course he owns it," the woman said in mocking tones. "He *is* the Reyes Corporation, Thaddeus. He told me that himself."

Lucas looked at her and saw what the problem was. Felix had bought this useless place. Now McDonough was dead, and his mistress, his lover, call her what you liked, was furious. She'd expected to inherit the property.

Greedy bitch.

A moment ago, he'd happily have solved his problem by donating El Rancho Grande to charity. Now, he knew he would fight this taunting female to the end to keep it— and then give it to charity.

"And you want it for yourself," he told her softly. "That's it, isn't it? That's the so-called 'stipulation.'"

"The ranch belongs to me," she said, drawing herself up. "By all that's right, that's legal, that's—that's human and decent, it's mine!"

"Of course it is, *amada*." Lucas's voice was silken. "Just think of all you did to earn it."

Her face colored. "You don't know what you're talking about!"

"I promise you, I do. I know the sacrifices you made, sleeping with an old man, doing his bidding in bed—"

"You—you disgusting son of a bitch! I'm going to take this damnable contract stipulation to court and I'll win."

"Do you have a million dollars? Because that is what it will cost you just to see me and my attorneys in a courtroom."

The woman glared at him. "You're more than pompous, Mr. Reyes. You're also a fool!"

Lucas took a step forward. The attorney moved quickly between him and the woman.

"Alyssa. Prince Lucas. My client is deceased but I'm honor-bound to continue representing him."

Norton's sudden show of backbone was a surprise but he had a point. There was a legal matter to be settled here, and Lucas wouldn't permit his anger at the rider to get in the way.

"Fine," he said coldly. "Then, let's get to the bottom line—or did we just reach it? Did you bring me all this distance to alert me to the fact that this woman is going to try to convince the courts the sale of the ranch was improper? That she should have inherited it? Because if that's the case, I must tell you, I suspect she has no legal grounds."

"I agree, sir. And that's not the problem."

"Then, what is?" *Dios,* he was tired. He wanted a meal and a shower and a night's sleep, but he damned well suspected he wasn't about to get them any time soon.

"Tell him, Thaddeus," the woman said.

Lucas looked at her. Her face was blank but hatred for him shone in her eyes.

Suddenly his exhaustion dropped away.

He thought of how he could change that look by taking her into his arms again and kissing her into submission. How she would respond to him. How she would beg him to make love to her.

Damn it, he thought, and strode to the window, stared into the black night while the wind shook the trees and the rain pelted the roof. He had nowhere to go until morning or, more precisely, he had no way to leave this place until then.

He had to calm down.

A deep breath. Then he turned to the attorney.

"She's right for once, Norton. Tell me the rest. I'm sure I'll find it amusing."

The lawyer pulled a handkerchief from his pocket and mopped his face.

"First, you must understand, sir. The ranch was not always the way it is today."

Lucas glanced at the photos on the wall. "So what? For all I give a damn, it might have been the finest ranch in all Texas."

"It was," the woman said in defiance.

"Fine. It was paradise. Just get on with it."

"A royal command, Thaddeus. You must obey."

Lucas glared at her. "Be careful, *amada*," he said softly.

"Yes, Alyssa, please. You're only making matters worse."

"You're the one making matters worse," she snapped. "If you'd done as I asked and simply ignored this whole thing—"

Lucas slammed his fist on the desk. So much for staying calm.

"Damn it," he roared, "that's it! Tell me what you're hiding about that contract, Norton, or so help me, I'll see you never practice law again!"

Thaddeus Norton took a briefcase from a chair and extracted a thick folder.

"Just bear in mind, sir, I told Aloysius this was insane."

"Insane?" The woman gave a shaky laugh. "How about immoral? Unethical? How about it's like something out of bad melodrama?"

"When the two of you get tired of this conversation," Lucas said coldly, "perhaps you'll be good enough to explain what in hell you're talking about."

The attorney opened his mouth and then shut it again. The woman shot him a look, then lifted her chin. She looked beautiful, proud and untouchable.

"Thaddeus is a coward, so I'll do it and then we can all have a good laugh. For starters… I hate to disappoint you, Mr. Reyes, but Aloysius wasn't my lover." She paused. "He was my father."

"You're McDonough's daughter?"

"His adopted daughter. My name was originally Montero. And there was never any warmth between Aloysius and me."

"Alyssa," Norton said wearily, "that's ancient history."

"You're right for once, Thaddeus, but our esteemed visitor wants answers. Well, I'm giving them to him. My mother is dead and so is Aloysius. I cannot imagine missing him, especially now that he's drawn me into this—this mess." Her smile was bitter. "Sorry this is all far less intriguing than me being the star of some sordid little drama, Your Mightiness, but that's the way it is."

"Let me get this straight," Lucas said in the tone of a man who'd just watched a rabbit pulled from a hat and knew damned well that sleight-of-hand tricks were not magic. "Aloysius McDonough learns he's dying. He has no wife but he has a daughter. She's cold and unfeeling and he has no desire to give her the land he once loved."

"Sounds good. And you've got it half-right, except the land was actually my mother's. And she loved it."

"Forgive me," Lucas said with heavy sarcasm. "I had the characters wrong but not the basic plot. You want the ranch. I own it. And? You got me here so you could do what? Beg me to give it back? Ask me to sell it to you for next to nothing?" His mouth twisted. "Or did you imagine you'd seduce me into giving it to you," he said, his eyes locked to hers. "Was that the plan?"

"Try 'none of the above,'" she said coldly.

"Really?" Lucas folded his arms. "I wasn't born yesterday, *amada.* Not being mentioned in Daddy's will must have been hard to accept."

"But I am mentioned. That's the problem."

"He left you something, then? Good for you but I don't see how it involves me, or why I've come such a distance to watch such a badly written play."

Was he wrong, or did some of her confidence seem to drain away?

"There's a clause in the contract. I didn't know about it until Aloysius died and the will was read. It's—it's what Thaddeus calls the stipulation."

"*Dios,* you say that as if the word might burn your mouth. Are you going to explain it, or must I shake it out of you?"

"I would advise against anything so foolish, Mr. Reyes."

That tough attitude was back. The statement was a challenge. So was the way she'd addressed him. His honorific creaked with antiquity in this century but her deliberate avoidance of it was, he knew, an insult.

Well, he wouldn't rise to the bait. He wanted the truth and he had the feeling it was worse than it seemed, more than one man scamming another out of a lot of money.

"Explain, then," he said gruffly.

Alyssa touched the tip of her tongue to her lips.

"Everything you've heard is true. My father offered this ranch to your grandfather, and your grandfather agreed to buy it. But—"

"But?"

"But," she said, her voice suddenly low, "your grandfather—your grandfather wanted to purchase something more. And my father agreed to sell it to him."

She fell silent as thunder roared over the house. The scent of ozone, of anticipation, hung in the air. A streak of jagged light sizzled just outside the window; thunder clapped overhead. It lent an air of melodrama to the scene.

And yet, Lucas thought, this was no melodrama. Whatever was playing out here was real.

Once, kayaking down a wild river, his craft had been poised at the lip of a class four rapid for what had seemed an eternity, enough time for him to look down into a whirl-pool he knew had claimed many lives.

His heart had missed a beat as he hung above it, caught somewhere between exhilaration and terror.

That was how he felt now, looking at Alyssa McDonough, waiting for her to finish telling him what he had come all this distance to learn.

"And?" he said softly. "What's the 'something more' your father agreed to sell to my grandfather?"

An eternity seemed to pass. Then Alyssa shuddered and raised her eyes to his.

"Me."

CHAPTER FIVE

THE look of horror on Lucas Reyes's handsome face was exactly what Alyssa had expected.

She recalled feeling just as horrified when Thaddeus first told her about what he kept calling the "stipulation."

"It's a joke," she'd insisted. "It's not legally binding. A clause like that is absolute nonsense."

"It isn't that simple," Thaddeus had said carefully. Marriage contracts, he explained, could be legal and binding. They were still in use in parts of the world, especially in royal families.

Alyssa had snorted with derision.

"I have news for you. We don't sell human beings in America."

"No one is selling a human being. I keep telling you, it's—"

"A marriage contract. It's still illegal. Tell Prince Felix I said so. And if he argues, tell him where he can shove that stipulation!"

"Read the contract before you make a decision, will you? It calls for the Reyes to restore the land and use it, in perpetuity, for ranching. Otherwise, the bank will seize it and you know what that means."

She knew, all right. A local developer was panting for all these rolling acres, eager to turn them into soulless tracts of cheap housing.

It was a sobering realization. Losing her mother's land was bad enough. Losing it to a developer was worse but being married off to a stranger…

"How could you have drawn up such a document?" she'd demanded.

Thaddeus admitted that he hadn't. Prince Felix's attorneys had done virtually all the legal work. He had done nothing but, in his words, crossed a few t's and dotted a couple of i's.

She was still groaning over that when he'd dropped the next bit of news.

Felix's grandson, the prince who would permit his grandfather to buy him a bride, was on his way to finalize arrangements.

"He's not finalizing anything!"

"The contract exists, Alyssa. I'm afraid there's little I can do."

"You can change it. Research it. Find precedents we can use to break it. I'll do the same. Damn it, I had a year of law school. I know there's not a contract written that can't be broken. How come you don't know that, too?"

"Read the contract," Thaddeus had repeated wearily.

So she'd read it. And the more she'd read, the more she'd seen just how cleverly the Reyes's lawyers had been in their use of language and tort law.

The contract seemed unassailable.

She'd sent Prince Felix a letter, demanding he forget the stipulation. She hadn't received an answer. She'd figured that meant the Spanish prince would not be dissuaded from coming to the ranch. Why? Was it to try to hold her to the contract terms? Did he actually think he could do that? Most of all, why would he be willing to marry a woman he had never seen?

The only thing that made sense was that Lucas Reyes was the human equivalent of a toad.

Squat. Bloated, with constant drool falling from fleshy lips. Ugly enough to frighten small children. Or tall. Skinny as a scarecrow, with ears that stood out from his head. After a couple of days, she'd decided he probably had warts, too.

And then she and Bebé had come within an inch of riding down a stranger. A tall, dark-haired, hot-eyed, gorgeous stranger…

The Spanish prince. And he had no idea who she was, or the real reason he was here. He honestly thought he'd come to look at a mare.

In reality, he'd come to look at her. Breeding stock, according to Aloysius.

Hadn't he always described her in the terms horsemen used when talking about mares? It started when she turned sixteen. She had, he'd said, good bloodlines. Good conformation. She'd make someone a good wife. Someone with money, who could infuse life back into the ranch was what he'd meant, though nobody dared say it.

A couple of months later, Aloysius had sent her east to boarding school, then college. She'd come home when her mother took ill, went east again after her death—and returned for the last time when Aloysius was dying. An act of human decency, because it had seemed the right thing to do.

Now here she was, staring at the stud she was supposed to be bred to.

The man who'd bought her from Aloysius.

So much for human decency.

Okay. Lucas Reyes hadn't bought her. He hadn't even known about the deal. Whatever. It was still humiliating and once she knew his identity, thanks to George, she'd phoned Thaddeus and demanded he drive over and handle things. She would stand by and listen, but Thaddeus would do the talking.

Wrong.

Thaddeus had taken the coward's way out. He'd tiptoed up to the truth, then lurched away from it so that she was stuck with the job. She'd have to explain why he was here to Lucas Reyes. It was horrible and demeaning and...

And, just look at the man. Look at His Mightiness. His jaw was trying its best to defy gravity.

He was—what was the word? Nonplussed. Alyssa wanted to laugh. His Mightiness, the Prince of Non-Plussed. It didn't even the score. She was still humiliated but at least he was completely bewildered.

How nice. How well-deserved.

He'd done a fine job of bewildering her this afternoon. Invading her space, forcing a confrontation...

Kissing her as if it was his right—but he probably thought it was. He was a prince, born to wealth and power and, okay, good looks.

Why not be honest?

Lucas Reyes was gorgeous.

Black hair. Hazel eyes. Strong jaw. A little dent in his nose that only heightened his sexiness.

He must have broken it sometime in the past.

A riding accident? Or an accident with a woman? It was nice to think some woman had given the prince her best shot.

The rest of the man was gorgeous, too. Long. Lean. Hard-muscled. When he'd kissed her she'd felt the masculine power of his body. The strength of it. When he'd kissed her...

God, when he'd kissed her…

Alyssa blinked. Lucas was looking at her with the intensity of a rattlesnake watching a field mouse.

It frightened her but she'd sooner have died than let him know it. She didn't know much about men—why would she want to? What she'd learned, watching her mother defer to Aloysius, was enough. But she knew stallions and to show weakness to a stallion was to put yourself in mortal danger.

So she steeled herself for the Spanish prince's inevitable questions and reminded herself that she'd had nothing to do with any of this, and he'd damned well better get that straight.

"Explain yourself."

His voice was low and filled with command. Alyssa narrowed her eyes. The last time anyone had used that tone with her was in sixth grade and Miss Ellison had demanded to know why she'd punched Ted Marsden in the nose.

Because he thought he could get away with putting his hand on my backside, she'd said, and Miss Ellison had tried, unsuccessfully, not to laugh.

Nobody was laughing now.

Alyssa drew herself up. "Excuse me?"

"I said—"

"I heard what you said. I just didn't like the way you said it."

Lucas stepped forward. She managed to stand her ground but was that really better than tilting her head back so she could keep her eyes on his?

"It's been a very long day, *amada,*" he said softly. "I am tired and irritable, I have not eaten since morning, and I am in no mood for nonsense."

"I'm sorry if you find our hospitality lacking," Alyssa said, her coolness making a mockery of the words, "but I am equally tired and irritable and, thanks to your presence, I have not eaten, either. Just knowing you were here spoiled my appetite."

She gasped as his hands closed around her shoulders.

"You are quick to offer insult."

"You are quick to show your temper."

"I want answers."

"And I want you gone. Perhaps, if we cooperate, we can both get what we want."

Angry as he was, Lucas almost laughed. *Dios,* this one was tough! Not that she wasn't frightened. Despite her show of bravado, he could feel her trembling under his hands.

Was she afraid of him?

He hoped not. She had angered him, yes. Infuriated him, was closer to the truth, but he had no taste for scaring women, especially women with such deep blue eyes and sweet, tender mouths.

And look how quickly she'd taken his thoughts from where they belonged, he thought coldly.

Something was going on here, a scam, a swindle of some kind, and he was not going to let this woman, who was surely part of it, distract him.

"That's the first intelligent thing you've said, *señorita.*" Lucas lifted his hands from her shoulders. "So, go on. Explain yourself. Oh. Sorry." A smile that wasn't a smile at all twisted his mouth. "What I meant," he said dryly, "is, would you kindly tell me what you meant by that cryptic statement? In what way did my grandfather supposedly 'buy' you?"

Alyssa decided to ignore his sarcasm. It was time to get this over with.

"As Thaddeus told you, your grandfather and my adoptive father signed a contract. Felix paid Aloysius half the agreed-upon price."

Lucas was watching her through narrowed eyes. "With the other half due when?"

"When the stipulation had been fulfilled."

"There's that word again."

Alyssa swallowed. A moment ago, she'd been ready to explain. Now—God, now, she just wanted the floor to open up.

"Well? I'm waiting. What 'stipulation'?"

"It's—it's… The stipulation involves—"

Her tongue felt as if it were glued to the roof of her mouth. How did you tell a man he was supposed to marry you?

"You see, Alyssa?" Thaddeus Norton's plump face was flushed. "It isn't that easy after all."

The lawyer marched across the room to Lucas and held out the folder he'd taken from his briefcase. A couple of minutes out of the line of fire seemed to have restored his courage.

"Read it yourself, Your Highness. In the end, it's simpler that way."

Lucas nodded, took the folder, extracted a sheaf of papers from it, turned his back to the room and began to read.

Half an hour went by.

Then he swung toward the attorney.

"This is insane."

"It's a marriage contract."

Lucas's face darkened. "Do not provoke me, Norton."

The lawyer's few seconds of courage seemed to be over.

"I'm not trying to provoke you, sir," he stammered, "I'm just stating the facts. That document—"

"Is a joke!" Lucas flung the pages on the desk and watched as they fluttered to the floor like dry leaves. "No one signs things like this anymore."

Alyssa nodded. "I said that. I told Thaddeus—"

"You told Thaddeus," Lucas said sharply. "Oh, I'll just bet you did!" His eyes narrowed. "Or did you dictate this to him line by line? Did you dip back into the middle ages and come up with a document guaranteed to send me into orbit?"

"Me?" She moved toward him, eyes flashing. "You think I…? Let me tell you something, Mr. Reyes—"

"It's Prince Reyes," Lucas snarled. "Or Your Highness. Get it straight."

"*I* had nothing to do with this, Your Mightiness. I didn't even know about it. Do you really think—do you honestly think I'd want my name linked to yours, even on a piece of paper?" She stopped an inch from him, hand lifted, forefinger pointed at the center of his chest. "Never! You understand that, oh almighty potentate? Not in a million years. Not in a hundred million years. Not ever!"

Lucas knew how to stop the angry words flying from that pretty mouth. All he had to do was haul her close, bury his hands in her hair and kiss her.

And, *Dios,* he wanted to do it.

To watch her eyes fill with rage—and then watch them fill with desire.

Was he crazy? He'd just read a document full of whereases and wherefores that boiled down to an arranged marriage between him and Alyssa Montero McDonough— that middle name made sense, he thought crazily, all that heat and smoldering fury—he'd just discovered his beloved, conniving, scheming, possibly senile grandfather had pledged his name and his fortune to a Texas wildcat, and he wanted to kiss her?

Like hell he did.

What he wanted was to get out of this madhouse. Not tomorrow. Right now.

"This," he said, "is getting us nowhere."

"A brilliant conclusion."

He shot her a look. "Do not push me," he said softly.

She started to speak, then obviously thought better of it. The woman wasn't a fool.

"I'm sure you and Norton thought this was very clever. I'm not sure how you managed it, how, exactly, you got my grandfather to sign this—this bit of legal mumbo jumbo—"

"Me?" Alyssa huffed. "*Me?* I didn't have a damned thing to do with it!"

"I had little to do with it, sir," Norton said, the words tumbling from his lips in a rush. "Your grandfather's attorneys did most of the work, then sent the papers to me, after which my client signed it in front of a notary and we sent it to Spain by messenger so that your grandfather could sign it, too, and then—"

Lucas pounded his fist on the desk again. By the end of this charade, he thought grimly, the damned thing would be fit for firewood.

"I have no interest in the back-and-forth steps, Norton! I'm talking about…" What was the phrase? Lucas had spent four years at Yale; he had a condo in New York. America was his second home but right now, his English was failing him. "I'm talking about the setup. The preparation you and McDonough and the charming Miss McDonough put into this—this sting."

"Sting?" Alyssa shot forward. This time, her finger almost poked a hole in his chest. "Your grandfather gets together with my father and they agree to—to sell me to you and you accuse *me* of a sting?"

She gasped as Lucas caught her wrist and yanked her arm behind her back. The action brought her to her toes. Brought her body suddenly against his.

His response was instantaneous. Just the feel of her, the

soft fragrance of her, and he hardened like stone. Her eyes widened in pretended innocence until they were big enough to swallow him whole.

"Isn't my reaction the desired effect, *amada?*" he said, so softly that only she would hear him. "Dangle the bait in front of the mark? Pretend innocence, then show outrage, and do it so well the poor sap believes it?"

"Hijo de una perra," she hissed through her teeth.

Lucas grinned and drew her closer.

"Don't be like that, *chica.* Just because I'm wise to you doesn't mean I don't find you appealing. But I'm not a fool. I don't buy my women—and if I did, I would not pay with my name and my fortune. That you thought I would insults my intelligence."

"What I thought," Alyssa said, her voice trembling, "was that you were too horrible to get a woman on your own. And, clearly, I was right."

She gasped as he tightened his hold.

"So horrible you kissed me as if you never kissed a man before? As if having me drink from your mouth is what you've waited for all your life?" His smile faded. "Or are you that fine an actress? Shall we try it again and see?"

"Prince Lucas," Norton said quickly, "please, sir, you've got this wrong."

The lawyer's voice quaked. He looked, Lucas thought with grim satisfaction, like a man watching a lighted match falling oh-so-slowly toward a box of dynamite.

"Miss McDonough—Alyssa is telling the truth. This was your grandfather's idea. And my client's," he added quickly.

"I find that difficult to believe."

"It's true, sir. Prince Felix can confirm it. Miss McDonough knew nothing about the arrangement until Aloysius's death."

"That's when you told her the happy news? That she would become a *princesa?*" Lucas smiled coldly. "But you're a bright girl, *amada.* You must have known how easily such good luck could slip through your fingers. How hard you must have worked to come up with a scheme that would keep me from getting away."

"Sir," Norton pleaded, "call your grandfather. Let him confirm my story."

"Why should I bother? I'm not going to honor this—this joke of a contract, Norton. You managed to defraud an old man, but—"

"Your grandfather paid half the sale price, Your Worship. Only half. And I did not—"

"Half is more than this desolate piece of land is worth." Lucas dropped Alyssa's wrist. She stumbled back, rubbing at the welt his fingers had left in her tender flesh. "You want more, sue us for it."

"I strongly urge you to phone Prince Felix," Norton said quietly. "I have no wish to sue you, sir, but I have an obligation to see my client's wishes to their rightful end."

The pudgy, small-town counselor, still shaken, seemed determined to stand his ground. That, more than anything, gave Lucas pause.

He'd already admitted, if only to himself, that Felix might have agreed to this nonsense. Not the marriage contract, of course. That, without question, was something McDonough or Norton or the woman had slipped into the agreement.

But Felix might have said he'd buy the ranch for twice its worth. He was an old man; he was not well; Aloysius McDonough had been his friend.

Why wait until he returned to Spain to ask Felix about the contract? He could get the answers he needed now and close the book on this mess.

If Felix said he had agreed to the purchase, Lucas would honor the contract terms. He'd write out a check and walk away.

The rest, the marriage agreement, the thing these two maniacs kept calling a stipulation, was a joke. He'd mention it to Felix if only for a laugh.

Lucas took his cell phone from his pocket. It was some ungodly hour of the morning back home but he didn't give a damn.

It was time to get to the bottom of this.

"Out," he commanded.

The attorney bolted. Alyssa stayed where she was, arms folded.

"This concerns me as much as you," she said coldly. "I'm not leaving."

Lucas inclined his head. "Stay, by all means, *chica,*" he said, just as coldly, "so I can see your face when my grandfather laughs at the supposed 'stipulation.'"

There were plenty of transmission bars now.

Lucas dialed his grandfather's private number. It rang a long time; the voice that finally answered was not a voice he knew.

"Who is this?" it said cautiously.

"Prince Lucas," Lucas snapped. "Who is this?"

"I am—"

Lucas heard snatches of unintelligible conversation, then Felix's familiar voice.

"Lucas?"

"*Si,* Grandfather. Who was that?"

"No one of importance. A new secretary. Where are you?"

"I am where you sent me. At El Rancho Grande…a misnomer if ever there was one."

"And what do you think, *mi hijo?*"

"I just told you. The place is in terrible condition. The outbuildings are falling down, the land is played out, there's no stock—"

"I know all that," Felix said impatiently. "What of the rest?"

"What rest, Grandfather? Do you mean the mare? There is no mare. There is nothing here except an attorney who insists we owe a final payment of twice what the land is worth and a woman who needs lessons in manners."

Silence. Then Felix gave a low laugh. "So her father told me, Lucas. The question is, are you the man to give them to her?"

The hair rose on the back of Lucas's neck. He turned toward Alyssa, still standing as she had been, back straight, arms folded, chin elevated at an angle so high it seemed impossible.

"*Abuelo,*" Lucas said softly, "what do you mean?"

"It's a simple question, *mi nieto.* Are you man enough to tame this mare?" Felix's tone turned sly. "Although my understanding is that my old friend's daughter is better described as a filly than a mare. Do you agree, Lucas?"

Lucas took the phone from his ear, stared at it as if he might see Felix's face if he tried hard enough, then sank down in a chair.

"You know about the marriage contract," he said, switching to Spanish.

"Of course."

"But why?"

"You know the reasons, Lucas. You are not getting younger."

"I am thirty-two." Yes, Lucas thought, but right now, he sounded twelve. "I am thirty-two," he said, more forcefully, "and before you make the speech you've made before, *si,*

I know of my responsibilities. I know it is my duty to carry on the Reyes name. I know—"

"Perhaps it is better to say, *I* am not getting younger."

"Grandfather…"

"She is of excellent stock. She is handsome. She is healthy." Felix's tone turned sly. "And I have been assured, she is a virgin."

Lucas shot another look at the woman. A virgin? A woman who burned like a flame in a man's arms? It was nothing but another lie.

"…ask, Lucas?"

Lucas cleared his throat. "I'm sorry, *abuelo*. I didn't get that. What did you say?"

"I said, what more could a man ask?"

"The right to make my own choices," Lucas said firmly. "I am sorry, Grandfather, *No voy a casar a esta mujer!*"

The words, "I am not going to marry this woman," seemed to echo through the room. He shot a sharp glance at Alyssa McDonough. Her expression had not changed. Of course not, he thought with relief. She didn't understand a word of his language.

"You are a grown man, Lucas. Do as you wish."

"Fine. I will see you tomorrow, then, in late—"

"You understand, you are not to pay the lawyer—the executor—the balance of the sale price for the ranch."

Lucas nodded. Felix was lucid. That, too, was a relief.

"Of course I understand. You overpaid the initial amount as it is."

"It was part of the arrangement, Lucas. Did you read the contract? If you did, read it again, more calmly this time, and you will see that if the marriage does not take place, we owe nothing more."

"Excellent."

"Yes. Just as long as you understand..." Felix coughed. The cough was deep and wet; it went on for a long time while Lucas frowned.

"Grandfather? Are you ill?"

Again, he heard muffled conversation. And, again, his grandfather's voice, not coughing now but somehow weaker.

"I am fine," the old man said briskly. "Where were we? Ah, yes. You will not give Thaddeus Norton the money."

"Trust me, Grandfather. I had no intention of it. As I said, you already gave them too much."

"It went to Aloysius. To pay for half the back taxes on the ranch. The bank will take the place now, to make up for the rest. There's a developer eager to plow all the acreage under."

"What the bank does is not our concern, Grandfather."

"I agree. The girl cares—she has some sentimental attachment to the land—but that, too, is not our concern."

Lucas looked at Alyssa again. Her face showed no emotion, but her eyes had the glitter of unshed tears.

Did she understand what he was saying? Who gave a damn? Not him. If she loved the place so much, why hadn't her father left it to her?

She was a good actress, that was all. Fiery when fire was needed, cold as ice when the situation demanded it.

And hot with passion when he kissed her, but was that part of the act? Yes. It had to be

Or had she surrendered to him? Surrendered to his kisses, his body, his need?

Furious with himself, Lucas stood, marched to the window and looked out. The storm had ended; a fat ivory moon was caught in the branches of a cottonwood tree outside.

"Well," Felix said, and sighed, "I did what I could. I told Aloysius the girl would not lose the land because, of course, once you married her and paid the arrears, the land would be, in a sense, as much hers as yours…but never mind."

Lucas rubbed his hand over his face. "Grandfather—"

"But I cannot force you to obey the terms of the contract, *mi hijo.* I understand that. It is a disappointment for me, that I cannot fulfill the wishes of my dead friend, but—"

"Grandfather. There must be a way around this."

"I am afraid there isn't. It's all right, Lucas. The girl is not your worry."

"No. She's not."

"She is her attorney's worry, and I am sure he will step in and help her. You have met him, have you not? Small man. Overweight. Soft. Sweats a lot."

Lucas turned and looked at Thaddeus Norton, who was mopping his forehead again.

"What about him?"

"Aloysius told me Norton has an, uh, an interest in the girl. A deep interest, if you know what I mean."

Dios, how could something simple become so complicated?

"Norton wants the woman for himself?" Lucas said, still speaking in Spanish, still watching Alyssa. Did her color heighten? No. It had to be his imagination.

"He does, yes. But it's the perfect solution. We don't pay the rest of the money, you don't get married. And the girl is taken care of. *Si?* The lawyer will see to it."

Lucas said nothing for several long seconds. Then he cleared his throat.

"Grandfather," he said briskly, "we entered into this arrangement in good faith."

"We? It was I, Lucas, not *we.*"

"Reyes entered into it," Lucas said, even more briskly. "So here's what I'm going to do. I'll tear up the contract, stipulation and all, and simply give her or the lawyer, whichever is appropriate, the money to pay off what is owed. She'll keep the ranch and we'll call it a gift in memory of an old friend."

"No."

Lucas raised his eyebrows. "No?"

"Aloysius and I entered into a contract."

"I understand all of that but, damn it…" He took a deep breath. "Look, we can well afford this—this act of charity, grandfather."

"Listen to me, Lucas. You must take another look at the contract. It is very specific. Unless the marriage takes place, there can be no final payment. The ranch is lost."

Lucas could feel a throbbing pain starting behind his left eye. No sleep. No food. No peace. No wonder his head hurt.

"Grandfather, maybe you didn't understand my suggestion. An act of charity—"

"I don't want your damned act of charity," Alyssa McDonough snapped.

Lucas stared at her. Had she understood the entire conversation?

Suddenly a cough rumbled through the telephone, and another and another. Lucas had never heard anyone cough like this; his grandfather sounded as if he were drowning.

"Grandfather? Grandfather!"

The coughing faded away and another voice came on the line.

"I'm sorry, Prince Lucas, but your grandfather cannot continue this conversation."

"What do you mean?" Lucas roared. "What's happening? Who in hell are you?"

"I am his nurse, sir, and—*Madre di Dios! Llamada para una ambulencia, Maria. Rapidamente!*"

The call ended in a blur of voices. Lucas struggled for control, then whirled toward Alyssa McDonough.

"I heard everything," she said. "Every word. I speak your language—were you too egotistical to think I couldn't? And I don't want your charity, I don't want anything from you, I don't want—"

"I must return to Spain immediately."

"Well, good for you because—"

"You will come with me."

"Don't be an ass!"

"I have no time to waste in foolish argument. There are issues to be settled and I cannot remain here to deal with them."

"Listen, you—you poor excuse for a human being—"

Lucas had spent part of an afternoon and most of an evening with this woman. She was still a stranger but he had learned one sure thing about her.

He knew how to silence her and he did, gathering her quickly in his arms, drawing her to him and taking her mouth, hard, with his.

She struggled.

He'd known she would.

And then she moaned, gave that little sigh he knew meant surrender, and lifted herself to him. To his kiss.

He gave in to it, if only for a second, to the pull of it, the sweetness, the hunger.

Then he clasped her shoulders and looked down into her blurred eyes.

"Will you walk, or must I carry you?"

"You can't do this!"

Lucas laughed, lifted Alyssa into his arms and carried her from the house.

CHAPTER SIX

WHAT made men think they had the right to walk right in and take over a woman's life?

Was it bred in their genes? Was there a strand of male DNA labeled "authoritative jerk?" Had scientists missed it all these years?

Maybe so.

Alyssa figured that would go a long way toward explaining the way her father—her adoptive father—had treated her mother. It would explain how he'd tried to treat her. How he *had* treated her, as it turned out, thinking he could sell her as if time had turned back hundreds of years.

She was being carried off by a stranger, an arrogant, unwelcome visitor in this house that should have been hers.

The feel of his arms closing around her stunned her, but not for long. When Lucas began striding from the room, her useless lawyer sputtering weak protests as he scurried after them, Alyssa's shock turned to fury.

"Hey!" she shouted. "What do you think you're doing?"

The Lord of the Universe didn't answer. He just kept walking toward the front door.

"Wait a minute!" Her voice rose higher. "I said—"

"I heard what you said." He shifted her weight, opened the door and stepped onto the porch. A chorus of crickets and tree frogs greeted his appearance. "At close to a thousand decibels, how could I not?"

The old wooden porch creaked as he walked across it and made his way down the steps. To where? Alyssa thought crazily, but the answer was obvious.

He was taking her to Thaddeus's black Cadillac.

The hell he was!

She kicked. She cursed. She pummeled his hard, unyielding shoulders. And she might have been an annoying mosquito, for all the response that got her.

"Damn it," she shrieked, "you can't do this!"

The prince dropped her to her feet beside the car.

"Norton. Give me your keys."

The command rang with authority. So did the pressure of the hand that kept her pinned to his side. Alyssa threw a desperate look at the lawyer who was watching the drama unfold with his pudgy mouth hanging open.

"Thaddeus," she said, "say something!"

Thaddeus stared at her. Then he cleared his throat.

"Your Highness. Your Majesty. Really, I don't think—"

"That's correct," Lucas said coldly. "You can't, or you would never have written that contract."

"I told you, it wasn't me, sir! It was your grandfather's people. Madeira, Vasquez, Sterling and Goldberg. Madrid, London, New York—"

"Spare me the roadmap, Norton. I know where they're located. Just give me your keys."

"Don't listen to him, Thaddeus!"

"She's right, sir. I mean, she could be right. About you not being able to do this. In fact, my legal opinion is—"

"He's useless," Lucas said to Alyssa. "If he weren't, you

wouldn't be in this fix to start with. His advice is the last thing you need."

"You just want me to lose the ranch!"

"You've already lost it, Alyssa. It's been sold. You have no claim to it any longer."

Her face heated. "Unless I marry you."

"There's no chance of that," Lucas said sharply. "If you think I'd let myself be ensnared in some old man's scheme…"

"You, ensnared? I'm the one who's trapped." Alyssa choked back a laugh. "It's like waking up and discovering you're starring in a bad old movie. The landlord. The maiden—"

"But no hero, *amada*. I refuse to be cast in that role." Lucas smiled unpleasantly. "As for the maiden… My grandfather might have fallen for the story of your supposed chastity but I'm not so easily fooled."

Color flooded her face. "Good. Because my chastity, or my lack of it, is none of your damned business!"

"I don't buy any of it, *chica*. For all I know, marrying me is precisely what you're after."

God, the insolence of the man! "You wish!"

Lucas grinned. "Ah, *amada,* you say that with such conviction."

"Just—just go away. Forget you ever came here."

"I would love to." A muscle knotted in his jaw. "I'd like nothing more than to walk away and know I'll never see you again."

"Do it. Turn around and start walking."

"I can't. My grandfather's lawyers wrote this damned contract because he wanted them to write it. Now he's ill." His voice roughened. "For all I know, he's dying. He made a commitment that matters to him and I'm not going to turn my back on it until I find a way out he can accept."

"You don't need to take me with you for that to happen."

"Unfortunately I do. I just explained the reason."

"You explained nothing!"

"This is a waste of time. Get in the car. Norton? For the last time, give me your keys." Lucas smiled coldly. "Unless you'd rather explain your part in all this to the Texas Bar Association."

It was a long shot. What did the lawyer have to explain, after all, except that he'd been unable to convince a dead man not to enter into an unenforceable contract?

But it worked. The attorney's face lost its color. Lucas saw it. So did Alyssa.

"Thaddeus," she said desperately, "Tell this—this lunatic that he can't do this!"

"This lunatic," Lucas said with some amusement, "is your only hope."

"You're not my hope! I'd sooner lose everything than marry you!"

"Haven't you been listening? You are not going to marry me! I am not going to be a sacrifice on the marriage altar."

"You, a sacrifice? What about me? This—this plan your horrible old grandfather hatched is—"

She gasped as Lucas grabbed her shoulders. "Watch yourself," he said softly. "And remember the bottom line. El Rancho Grande is at the heart of this situation."

"You don't give a damn about the ranch."

"You're right, *amada,* I don't." His expression hardened. "But my grandfather says you do. And, in honor of his commitment to an old friend, so does he." His mouth flattened. "That puts finding a way out of this mess squarely in my hands."

Alyssa's head was spinning. Refuse to go with Lucas

and the land was gone. Go with him and maybe, only maybe, it could be saved.

"This," she said shakily, "this has—it has become very complicated."

Lucas gave a bark of laughter.

"What if I agree to go with you? What will happen?"

"I'll convince my grandfather that the contract is unenforceable, write a check for the arrears and the balance of the mortgage, deed the ranch to you and pretend we never met."

She stared at him. "Can you do all that?"

He damned well hoped he could but she didn't want to hear his doubts any more than he did.

"Yes," he said, with more conviction than he felt.

"And you'll start by abducting me."

"This is hardly an abduction, *chica*. After all, you are my betrothed. It says so in that damnable stipulation."

"This isn't a joke! I'm not your anything and you know it."

"You're right. And I'm wasting time. So, decide, *amada*. Stay here or go with me. I'm tired of this discussion."

Alyssa opened her mouth to argue but argue about what? The damnable prince was right. They'd already talked the problem half to death and neither of them was any nearer a certain solution than before.

She looked at Thaddeus. He was right about that, too. Her father's lawyer was useless.

"Yes or no, *amada?* Do I leave you here, or do you come with me?"

A cloud drifted across the face of the moon, momentarily obscuring everything but Lucas Reyes's hard face. Alyssa shuddered as if the warm Texas night had suddenly turned cold.

This enigmatic stranger had invaded her life. He was all

but convinced she'd known about the contract. That she wanted to marry him for his money and his title.

That she was, in other words, sly, scheming and greedy.

What would he say if she told him she'd been heart-broken when she'd learned the land wouldn't be hers? That it was all she had left of her mother? That seeing the soil paved over, the old barns and stables knocked down to make room for what some called progress, would break her heart all over again?

Foolish question.

Lucas Reyes would say nothing. He wouldn't believe her.

And why should she believe him? He said he was taking her with him because he wanted to convince his grandfather the contract couldn't be enforced but was that true? Why would a man take a woman thousands of miles from her home for that reason?

Why should she trust him?

He could do anything to her, with her, once she left the safety of her home, her country…

"Well?"

His expression was still remote, his eyes flat pools of darkness. He was beautiful and terrifying and just the thought of all his power, all his intensity focused on her made her blood start to race.

Tears burned her eyes. She blinked them back. Her only defense was to convince him she wasn't afraid of him.

"If I were to go with you," she said, trying her best to sound calm, "you'd have to agree to certain—"

"Stipulations?"

His voice was soft as velvet but there was a razor-sharp edge to the implied humor in the word.

"Conditions," she said. "Certain conditions."

"Such as?"

"Such as, you are to treat me with respect."

A negligent shrug. "Done."

"And you are not to touch me."

He laughed.

"You think this is funny? That you can—that you think you can kiss me whenever you want?"

"I think you demand too much." His eyes went cold. "Too many conditions, provisos, stipulations, whatever. Come with me or don't."

A tremor went through her. Going with him was wrong. It was crazy. It was—

"Norton! The keys, man. Or I'll take them from you."

The keys arced through the darkness and into Lucas's waiting hands.

"Decision time, *amada*. I'm leaving, with you or without you."

Her feet wouldn't move. Lucas shrugged and got behind the wheel.

"Even if—even if I wanted to go with you," she said, rushing the words together, "I couldn't until—until I got my things."

"What things?"

"Clothes. My toothbrush. Things," she said, hating the desperation in her voice.

"I will arrange for you to get everything you need when we reach my country."

It was the kind of arrogant response she should have expected.

"My handbag, then. My wallet. My ID. Won't I need a passport?"

He laughed. Why wouldn't he? Even she had to admit it was impossible to think that a woman traveling with this man would need anything so mundane.

"Last chance," he said, reaching over the console and opening the passenger door. "Yes or no?"

Alyssa ran the tip of her tongue over her dry lips.

He made it sound as if she had a choice but they both knew she didn't. She hated him as much for that as for kissing her, for making her dizzy with his kisses...

The sound of the Caddy's powerful engine idling in the still night filled her with dread. Her heart bumped into her throat.

Quickly, knowing that thinking about it too long might be a mistake, she slid into the passenger seat and shut the door after her.

"Just be sure you understand one thing." Her voice trembled and she hated showing that little sign of weakness. "If there were any other way, I wouldn't go with you."

"Duly noted, *amada,*" he said, with a tight smile, "if not fully believed."

God, she wanted to launch herself across the console and hit that square, impertinent jaw but that would have been stupid and she knew it. Instead she looked out the window, saw Thaddeus's incredulous face and then the car was moving forward, gaining speed as it left the house and the attorney behind.

"Alyssa?"

Lucas sounded so calm. Had he realized this was all a terrible mistake? Was he human after all? Was he going to apologize for how he'd behaved?

"Yes?"

"Is there a better way to get to the local airport than the road I was on this morning?"

So much for wishful thinking. Bitterness made her incautious.

"The road where you made an ass of yourself, you mean?"

He stood on the brakes and the car skidded to a halt in a cloud of dust. He swung toward her, his face cold and hard in the light from the dashboard.

"I will not tolerate insolence."

"And what about what *I* will not tolerate? Your vicious assumptions. Your—your pathetic attempts at seduction…"

She was in his arms before she could protest. He took her mouth with his as he had those other times, hard, deep, fast. He kissed her as if the contract was valid and she was his.

Suddenly the shock of what was happening overwhelmed her.

Alyssa began to weep.

She cried without sound, tears trailing down her face. She tasted the salt of them on her lips and he must have, too, because all at once, his kiss changed.

His mouth softened, asked instead of demanded. He whispered her name against her lips.

And her bones felt as if they might liquefy.

No, she thought, I don't want this.

"Si, amada," he whispered, "you do."

Alyssa had spoken the thought but it didn't matter because Lucas was drawing her into his lap. She could feel the beat of his heart, the power of his erection.

And then she stopped thinking.

She leaned into him. Let his arms enfold her, his hard body take the weight of hers. She had stood alone for so long. For all of her life. To surrender to his strength, to give herself up to him…

A whimper broke from her throat.

His hands cupped her face. She covered them with hers and he tilted her head back, changed the angle of their kiss. Her lips parted, clung to his. His taste was on her tongue, clean and heart-stoppingly male.

Her body was singing.

Singing, and aching for more than this kiss. For more, oh God, more…

He whispered something in Spanish. She felt his mouth at the pulse point beating rapidly in her throat, felt his hands sweep down her body, beneath her leather jacket and skim her breasts, his thumbs barely brushing her nipples.

Sensation shot through her. She cried out, arched against him. Her head fell back and he bent his head, kissed her silk-covered nipple, closed his teeth lightly around it.

Another cry burst from her throat. She buried her hands in his hair and he said her name as he slid his hand down the back of her trousers, under the edge of her panties. His palm burned against her skin.

God!

She wanted this, wanted more, wanted—

Suddenly Lucas tore his mouth from hers. Her eyes flew open as he thrust her back into her own seat. She saw his face.

His cool, amused face.

"So much for my so-called pathetic attempts at seduction, *chica.* As for your response… Very nicely done. It's everything a man could want in a woman. Sweet. Passionate." The look of amusement fled. "And, unfortunately, a little too convincing. I cannot imagine a virgin would return a kiss with such fervor."

Alyssa lunged at him, fist raised. Lucas wrapped his hand around hers, hard enough to make her wince.

"You can understand, then, if I inform you that your comments about seduction strike me as a tease rather than a complaint."

She spat a word at him, and he laughed.

"Such language, *amada,* and from that supposedly innocent mouth." His laughter faded; his eyes turned cold.

"As for seduction... If you behave yourself, I might consider taking you to bed. But I wouldn't marry you if you were the last woman on earth. Is that clear?"

Alyssa yanked her hand free. "You're despicable."

"You break my heart."

"You don't have a heart!"

"All I want from you is help convincing my grandfather that this contract should never have been written, not for your sake or mine but for his. He is old and I love him, and I would not hurt him for the world. Do you understand?"

She wanted to make a clever response but her brain didn't seem to be working.

Lucas Reyes was a mass of contradictions.

She'd accused him of having no heart but he did, when it came to his grandfather. But when it came to everything else... How could he kiss her and fake all that passion?

Better still, how could she have responded to him when she hated him?

"Now," he said coolly, "I ask you again. Is there a better road to the airport?"

She wanted to tell him the road to hell was the best road for him, but she wasn't stupid.

Lucas Reyes was the enemy but for now, it would be best not to take him on. Instead she kept her voice as toneless as possible.

"Take the left fork at the end of the driveway, then the first road after that."

"And where will I end up, *amada?* On my way to the airport—or on my way to hell?"

The look on her face made Lucas want to laugh.

But he didn't.

Reading Alyssa McDonough's thoughts was easy—but there was little to laugh about tonight.

His grandfather lay ill. He was bringing home a woman he distrusted. Who knew what was truth and what was deceit? Finding the answer seemed as elusive as chasing moonlight.

And, come to think of it, how was he going to get home? His plane would not be waiting for him. He'd sent it to New York, hours ago.

Lucas's jaw tightened. *Madre de Dios,* what a mess!

He dug out his cell phone, mentally crossed his fingers and flipped it open. Four transmission bars appeared. Four beautiful, big transmission bars. Quickly, before the gods of mischief could erase them, he punched in 4-1-1 and asked for the airport's number.

Luck stayed with him.

The office was open. And yes, there was a plane available for rent and yes, its range was sufficient to get to New York City.

Lucas made the necessary arrangements, phoned his pilot in New York, told him to be ready to go as soon as they arrived at JFK. When he flipped the phone shut, he found Alyssa watching him.

"Do people always do as you tell them?"

It was a cool statement, not a question, and he knew better than to take her words as a compliment. Instead he leaned across the console, caught her face in his hand before she could pull away and took her mouth in a slow, deliberate kiss.

"Si," he said softly, "always."

Then he swung the car back onto the road and gunned the engine.

CHAPTER SEVEN

THEY left Texas in the small jet Lucas had rented, his hand firmly on Alyssa's elbow as they boarded, as if he thought she might bolt at the last minute.

The truth was, she thought about it but stubbornness and pride kept her moving up the steps and into the plane.

Backing down now would have been a sign of weakness.

In New York, they boarded his own plane. She'd expected something like the jet they'd flown from Texas, a small, handsome craft with a handful of seats.

She should have known better.

Lucas's plane was enormous, a sleek silver bird outfitted in glove-soft black and beige leather.

Though she'd lived in New York long enough to know that men who headed up international corporations often traveled in corporate jets and saw them not simply as perks but as necessities, she refused to think that of Lucas.

The way he treated her, his easy assumption that he could walk into her life and take it over and now the luxurious plane, even the presence of a steward, seemed proof that the Spanish prince saw himself as better than the rest of the world.

She didn't like this man. Didn't trust him. That she'd

been susceptible to his advances didn't just embarrass her, it angered her.

He'd sensed how naive she was and made the most of it.

Not anymore, she thought as the steward served dinner on fine china that bore a royal crest.

Now, she had a plan.

Eating the meal set before her was part of it. Maybe the steak and salad, the coffee and brie and water biscuits were the equivalent of breaking bread with the enemy but she had to maintain her strength.

Lucas would be a formidable opponent in what she increasingly saw as a complex chess game.

He had made the first move and he thought he had command of the board.

He didn't.

As soon as they reached Spain, she'd tell him he had three days to settle this thing. That was more than enough time to convince an old man that he stood to lose more than he'd gain by interfering in two lives.

Playing God was never a good idea, and Prince Felix Reyes had to understand that.

Three days. Then she was going home.

One year of law school hadn't turned her into a legal hotshot but even a novice could see that this contract had holes big enough to swallow a truck.

She'd go to New York, see her former professors. Surely one would give her the advice she needed.

Already, she could see the bare bones outline of how to fight the sale of the ranch.

Aloysius's body had wasted away. Toward the end, so had his mind. Who knew how long that had been going on? Had he been mentally capable when he'd sold the ranch? When he'd agreed to an unenforceable stipulation?

Maybe Felix Reyes had lied to him about what he was signing. Maybe Thaddeus had gone along with it, or maybe he'd simply been bowled over by a high-powered international law firm.

The bottom line was that the contract didn't make sense. Why would Felix Reyes have wanted such played-out land? Why would he have wanted her for his grandson?

Lucas could surely have all the women he wanted.

Alyssa finished her coffee, put down the delicate cup and saucer and glanced over at him, seated in a leather armchair across the aisle. His meal lay untouched on the table in front of him. His hands were wrapped around a heavy crystal glass that held an inch of amber liquid; his face was to the window.

Despite what she knew of him, what she thought of him, her pulse gave an unwelcome little kick.

He was so incredibly beautiful.

Tall. Dark. Masculine. And, ever since they'd changed planes in New York, quiet and brooding.

In fact, to her relief, he'd ignored her. He spent most of the time on the plane's satellite phone, speaking sometimes in English, sometimes in Spanish, his voice never loud enough for her to pick up more than a couple of words but enough so she knew his conversations were about his grandfather.

She almost found herself feeling sorry for him. She'd even come close to leaning over and—and what? Telling him everything would be okay? Offering her compassion?

What compassion had he offered her? He was a cold-hearted, manipulative tyrant, clearly accustomed to having his own way.

Lucas turned and looked at her. His eyes were very dark; the bones in his cheeks seemed more pronounced than usual. She could see that he was hurting…

Alyssa broke eye contact.

Three days. A second more was to court disaster.

In midafternoon, the jet began a smooth descent through a bright blue sky, touched down on a long ribbon of concrete and finally braked to a gentle stop.

Green meadows bracketed the landing strip; on a distant rise, a herd of horses stood silhouetted against a lush backdrop of leafy trees.

A black Rolls-Royce sped along a parallel road and stopped; two men in coveralls began wheeling a mobile staircase to the plane as the steward entered the cabin and opened the outside door.

"Welcome home, Your Highness," he said pleasantly.

Alyssa rose to her feet. So did Lucas, who clasped her shoulder as she started past him.

"Wait."

An imperial command. Did he think she was one of his subjects? She shrugged off his hand, brushed past the steward...

And almost tumbled into the yawning gap between the plane and the mobile stairs.

A strong arm wrapped around her waist and pulled her back.

"Madre de Dios," Lucas said sharply, "what in hell were you doing?"

"I thought—the door—I thought—"

She was shaking like a leaf. So was he. Another step and...

Lucas cursed, turned Alyssa to him and gathered her tightly in his arms. He half expected her to resist but she collapsed against him, heart pounding against his, breath quick and shallow.

"Lyssa." He shut his eyes, buried his face in her hair. "It's my fault. The stairs—"

Alyssa shuddered. "There were no stairs."

"*Si.* I know."

"*It* was my fault entirely, sir," the steward said in a shaken whisper. "If I hadn't opened the door—"

"No, it's not your doing, Emilio." Lucas cupped Alyssa's face and lifted it so he could look into her eyes. "Emilio knows I always want the door opened as soon as possible. I like the smell of home. The grass. The sea beyond the hills. The horses." *Dios,* her face was so pale! "Now you will think I am a crazy man, admitting I love the smell of horses."

His attempt at calming her seemed to work. A hint of color rose in her cheeks and she gave a choked laugh.

"The only crazy person here is me, trying to walk on air."

The steps locked into place with a metallic thud.

"We can toss a coin to decide the winner later." Lucas's smile faded. "Are you all right, *chica?*"

"Yes. I'm—I'm fine."

Not true. He could feel her heart doing the *paso doble* and she was still trembling. Letting go of her was out of the question, and he swung her up into his arms.

"Lucas. Really. I can walk."

"*Si.* So can I. Humor me, *amada.* Put your arms around my neck and let me carry you to the car."

He didn't wait for her answer. Instead he crossed the grassy ribbon between the landing strip and the shiny black Rolls-Royce waiting on the blacktop. The driver saluted.

"Welcome home, Your Highness."

"Thank you, Paolo."

Lucas bit back a grin.

Paolo, normally the most unflappable of souls, was

having a difficult time trying not to stare but then, the sight of his employer with a woman in his arms was not an everyday occurrence.

It was not an occurrence that had taken place here at all.

Lucas had never brought a woman to the *finca*. It was his by birthright but it was also Felix's home, and he always exercised discretion where his grandfather was concerned...

Dios. Another problem, one he had not considered. Paolo would not be the only one of the household staff to be shocked at the sight of Alyssa. All of them would undoubtedly leap to the same conclusion, that he had finally decided to bring a mistress home with him.

He couldn't let that happen.

This was Spain. Princes still did not have to explain themselves to anyone but that rule didn't apply to young women, not in the world in which old bloodlines and older conventions still ruled.

"Paolo," he said gently.

The chauffeur blinked. "Sorry, sir. I, ah, I, ah—"

He swung open the rear door of the Rolls-Royce and Lucas slipped into the seat, Alyssa still in his arms. She struggled a little; his arms tightened around her and he put his lips to her temple.

"Sit still, *amada*," he whispered.

"Your driver will think—"

"Worry about what *I* will think, if you keep shifting against me that way."

The soft taunt had the effect he'd anticipated. Alyssa blushed and went very still just as Paolo got behind the wheel.

"This is Señorita McDonough," Lucas said.

"Señorita," Paolo said, smiling at her in his mirror.

"She will be visiting with us for a while."

"Yes, sir."

Lucas frowned. He'd have to come up with something better than that but for now…

For now, his thoughts returned to what mattered most. Felix.

"Has there been any change in my grandfather, Paolo?"

"None I have heard of, sir."

No. There wouldn't have been. Lucas had phoned endless times, spoken with doctors and nurses, with something called a patient liaison, and each had told him the same thing.

No change. Felix was still in a coma.

"Do you wish to go to the hospital, sir?"

"Take us to the house first. I'll get the *señorita* settled in and then I'll go to the hospital."

"I don't need settling in," Alyssa hissed. "And I wish you'd let go of me! What will the chauffeur think?"

Lucas looked at the firebrand in his arms. Her face was flushed, her hair had long ago come loose of its demure knot and whatever lipstick she'd had on was worn away by the endless hours since they'd left Texas…

Kissed away by his mouth on hers.

"You cannot just—just march around carrying me as if I were—as if I were—"

Bending his head, he kissed her, felt her initial struggle fade and become acquiescence, felt her lips soften, felt the sweetness of her sigh.

When he looked up, he caught Paolo openly gaping at them in the mirror.

"Paolo," he said gently, "I forgot to mention…"

"Sir?"

"Señorita McDonough has done me the honor of agreeing to become my wife."

* * *

"Are you out of your mind?"

They were the first words Alyssa had spoken since Lucas's impossible announcement.

He'd carried her from the car, up a set of steps and through the massive doors of what could only be called a mansion, past a butler, a housekeeper, a maid, past half a dozen people who stared at her, at him, then beamed when he made the same announcement to each.

This is Señorita McDonough. Mi novia.

His fiancée. His fiancée, when in reality she was a woman who wanted to claw his eyes out.

But she'd kept quiet, knowing anything she said would be pointless, that the arrogant Spanish prince would shut her up by kissing her.

Once they were alone, she'd tell him what an idiot he was.

And they were alone now.

He'd carried her up an elegant, curving staircase, down a wide hall, shouldered open a door, kicked it shut behind him and, at last, dropped her on her feet. Then he'd folded his arms and looked at her in a way that said he knew what was coming next.

"All right, *amada,*" he'd growled, "let's have it."

And she'd given it to him. A look of rage, of disbelief, and then the question that was really a statement.

"Are you out of your mind?"

He had to be. Why else say they were engaged? Why further complicate something that was quickly becoming impossible?

He scowled. Glared. Ran his hands through his dark hair until it stood up in little ruffles. He paced across the room, swung around, faced her and said, "I had no choice."

"You had no choice?"

"That's correct. I had no—"

"You told everyone—everyone!—that I'm your fiancée because you had no choice?"

"*Chica.* If you would calm down—"

"We both agreed that contract, that inane stipulation, is a joke. It's why I said I'd come here with you, because we agreed. Because you said you'd find a way to make your grandfather see it was wrong."

"Unenforceable."

"Unenforceable, wrong, what's the difference?" Alyssa slapped her hands on her hips. "I knew I shouldn't have believed you!"

His face darkened. "Are you calling me a liar?"

"You just told your staff that we're engaged. What would you like me to call you? Creative? Inventive?" Alyssa blew a lock of hair out of her eyes. "I did a lot of thinking today. Tonight. Whatever you call it when you fly through umpteen time zones."

"Three time zones," Lucas said coolly. "I know it's difficult but try to be accurate."

"Four, counting this one, and that's not the point!" She strode toward him, eyes hot. "And now, here you are, telling your staff, telling the entire world that I am something I most definitely am not."

Lucas folded his arms. "Are you finished?"

"No, I am *not* finished. If you think, if you for one second think I would ever agree to the terms of that—that stipulation—"

"Amazing, how you make that into a dirty word."

"I wouldn't marry you if—if—"

"If I were the last man on earth. A cliché, *amada,* but why worry about such things when you're in the middle of a tirade?"

He was right. She was ranting and what was the point?

Hadn't she spent hours coming up with a plan? Well, with parameters for *his* plan, the one that involved making his grandfather see the light?

Alyssa took a deep breath.

"The point is—"

"The point," Lucas said grimly, stalking toward her, grabbing her by the shoulders, hoisting her unceremoniously to her toes, "the point, my charming *novia,* is that you have nothing to worry about. I would not marry you, either, not if you were the last female in the universe!"

"Then why—"

"Because," he growled, lowering his head so their eyes met, "because I am a fool who suddenly realized that bringing you here could ruin your reputation."

She opened her mouth, then shut it. Her reputation? This man had insulted her, threatened her, bullied her, accused her of lying about being a virgin, and now he was worried about her reputation?

He had to be joking.

"I admit, I should have thought of it sooner."

"Thought about my reputation," Alyssa said slowly.

"Yes. This is a small place. A world unto itself."

"What small place? What world?"

"This one," he said with impatience. "Andalusia. Those who live here. Those who breed these horses."

"*I* don't live here. And, as you surely know, *I* don't breed horses, Andalusians or otherwise." Her mouth thinned. "Not anymore."

"But you did."

"Once, a very long time ago, my mother bred them."

"And so will you, once I find a way to break the contract and return the land to you."

Her heart lifted. That was what he'd said he wanted to

do, to his grandfather during their phone call and then to her. Did he actually mean it?

"Trust me, *amada*. It is a small world we live in. You don't want people talking about you. I have no right to permit people to assume I need you here for—for the wrong reasons."

"You mean," she said coolly, "a man like you needs women for only one reason."

"Yes. No! Damn it, Lyssa—"

"You called me that before. It isn't my name."

"What in hell does what I call you have to do with what we're discussing?"

Alyssa blinked. What were they discussing, exactly? She wasn't sure anymore. Lucas was standing too close. His hands on her shoulders were too warm. His eyes were too dark.

"I like the name Lyssa," he said, his voice softening. "It suits you. Does it bother you that I call you by it?"

Bother her? Why would it? The way he said it, *Lyssa*, as if he were whispering it to her. As if it belonged only to them. As if they were alone together, their mouths fused, their bodies on fire…

Oh God!

"No," she said coolly, "no, it doesn't bother me at all. Anyway, you're right. It has nothing to do with what we were talking about."

"Reputations."

"Yes."

"Well, the point is…" Lucas cleared his throat. "The point is, the sight of you disconcerted my people."

"You mean," she said sweetly, "they're not accustomed to seeing you carry home the spoils of war?"

"They're not accustomed to seeing me bring a woman

into this house," he said, refusing to be sidetracked. "I've never done it before."

Why did that make her want to smile? "You haven't?"

"That's what I just said, *amada*. No, I have not. And I suddenly realized my people would—well, they would see you and come to the wrong conclusion." He cleared his throat. "I don't want them to think I brought you here for sex."

"So, I was right. You're concerned about your own rep—"

"Damn it," Lucas growled, "that's not it! You've been through enough. Why should anyone pin a label on you because of me?"

Alyssa blinked. Maybe there was a heart buried under all that macho muscle.

"That's—that's very kind, but—"

"Let everyone think you're my *novia*. It will protect you from gossip." His mouth twisted in a rueful smile. "Trust me, *amada*. Gossip travels, even from one side of the Atlantic to the other."

"Well—well, as I said, that's kind of you. But—"

"At the end of all this, I'll simply say we decided our engagement was a mistake."

She nodded. "Of course," she said, and wondered why what he'd said should make her feel a little sad.

Lucas nodded, too. "I'll tell Dolores to come up and see you. Let her know what you need."

"Everything," Alyssa said, with a little laugh. "Clothes. A toothbrush. A comb. A shower—"

"I can take care of that."

His voice was suddenly low and husky. She looked up and caught her breath at what she saw in his eyes.

"The clothes, I mean," he said softly. "I'll take you with me tomorrow. You can buy whatever you wish."

"I couldn't—"

"Of course you could." He smiled; one hand cupped her chin and he traced her lips with his thumb. "I carried you off, *amada*. I owe you much more than a shopping trip."

"Lucas—"

"You see? My name is not so difficult to say after all."

"Lucas." God, her head was swimming. She'd been furious at him just a little while ago. Now, all she could think of was how dark his eyes were. How the brush of his thumb felt on the curve of her lip. "Lucas. On the plane… I was thinking—"

Slowly he drew her to him. "*Sí.* So was I."

"About—about our situation."

"I, too, *amada*." He smiled. "I was thinking how very glad I am that the contract stipulation did not involve a woman like the one my cousin Enrique found himself betrothed to."

"We're not betrothed," Alyssa said, and wondered at how breathless she sounded.

"No. Certainly not. But Enrique was." His smile became a grin. "His *novia* outweighed him."

Alyssa laughed softly. "You're making that up."

"Cross my heart," Lucas said, trying to look serious. "And she had only one eyebrow." He put his finger to his temple and drew a line straight across his forehead. "One thick, black eyebrow. Can you imagine?" Slowly, inexorably, he drew her into his embrace. "Only a very fortunate man finds himself in a marriage contract with a woman as beautiful as you, *chica*."

"It isn't a real contract," Alyssa said quickly.

"Of course not. But if it were—"

"It isn't," she said again and this time it was she who rose on her toes, who offered her mouth for Lucas's kiss.

He kissed her gently at first. Tenderly. Gathered her in his arms as if she were fragile as glass…but it wasn't enough.

Not for him.

Not for her.

"Lucas," she whispered, and he groaned and enveloped her in his arms, his kiss deepening, heating, and she responded to it, pressed herself against him, touched the tip of her tongue to his.

His hands slid down her spine.

He cupped her bottom. Lifted her into him. Into his erection. And when she gasped, he said something against her mouth and suddenly he was holding her as if she were a woman, not a delicate bit of crystal.

His hands swept under her skirt, up her legs, and she moaned and thrust her hands into his hair, lifting herself to him, telling him with every beat of her heart, every whisper of her breath, that she wanted him.

"Amada," he said thickly, and he slid a hand between her thighs, cupping her, feeling her heat, hearing her sharp little cry of pleasure, feeling her dampness against his palm. Then she was in his arms again and he was carrying her quickly through the gathering shadows of late afternoon, through another door, to a bed, a four-poster bed hung with ivory lace…

Someone pounded on the sitting room door.

Lucas lifted his head. Lyssa was still in his arms, her eyes blurred with desire, her lips rosy and swollen from his.

The fist hit the door again.

"Sir! Your Highness! The hospital called. Your grandfather… He's conscious."

It took a moment to register. He had forgotten everything but the woman in his arms. The sorceress who had the power to dazzle him even though he still didn't know if she was a good witch or an evil one.

He lay her on the bed. Then he bent over her and kissed her again, hard enough to make her gasp, hard enough to nip her flesh...

Hard enough to leave his brand on her body as well as her soul.

Alyssa rolled onto her belly as he hurried from the room. She wrapped her arms around the pillow, her breathing quick, her pulse roaring in her ears. Her mouth still tasted of Lucas's; his scent was on her skin.

Another minute and she'd have given herself to him.

She moaned softly, shut her eyes and buried her face in the pillow.

She'd been wrong to let him bring her here but that could be remedied. She would leave him. Leave this place...

Except, she had no money. No passport. She had nothing but her anger and it stayed with her, made her leave the bed, shower, put on the same clothes she'd been wearing for what seemed forever, speak curtly to Dolores when the housekeeper knocked an hour later to see if she was all right.

"I'm fine," she snapped, and Dolores stammered out an apology for interrupting and left.

Alyssa felt as if she were coming apart. What she'd almost done, what she'd almost let Lucas do, proved it. Surely she'd never have melted into him if she were functioning normally.

She had not slept in hours. In days, or so it felt. She was beyond exhaustion; she knew that, but she couldn't seem to stop pacing while she planned what she would say to Lucas when he returned.

She remembered the night Aloysius had died. How she'd stood beside his still form and felt nothing. How, hours later, the tears had finally come, tears for what might have been.

This was different. She knew that.

And, as late afternoon became evening, she began wondering what Lucas was facing in a hospital room at the side of an old man he so obviously loved.

Night fell over the Reyes mansion. Stars blazed in new constellations of fierce fire against the pitch-black sky. The adrenaline that had kept her going suddenly drained away, leaving her spent and weary.

She stripped off her clothes, leaving them where they fell, wrapped herself in a soft white cotton robe she found in the closet and stumbled to the bed.

Long hours later, a whisper roused her from the depths of sleep.

"Lyssa?"

Alyssa forced her eyes open. Lucas was sitting on the bed beside her, limned by moonlight, weariness and despair etched in every line of his proud, beautiful face.

He stroked his hand over her hair.

"Forgive me for being gone so long, *chica*. But my grandfather—"

"Is he—?"

"He's alive," he said in a low voice, "but—"

He shook his head. Without thinking, she reached up and touched his cheek.

"I'm sorry, Lucas."

"*Si*. Thank you for that."

Alyssa looked up at him in silence. Then, slowly, she reached for him. On a soft groan, he gathered her close and stretched out beside her.

"Go to sleep, *amada*," he whispered, and she sighed, put her head on the shoulder of the arrogant, hard-hearted Spanish prince and took him with her deep, deep into sleep.

CHAPTER EIGHT

IN THE deepest hours of darkness, a night-creature called from the jasmine-scented gardens below the bedroom window. Its cry was soft, but it was enough to draw Lucas from his sleep.

He frowned into the darkness.

What bed was this? Not his. Neither was the room. For a second, he thought he was in New York, in his penthouse on Central Park West...

Until he felt the delicate weight of the woman in his arms.

Alyssa.

She was sprawled half-over his body, her thigh across his, her arm lying over his chest. Her head was on his shoulder; silky strands of her hair drifted across his lips.

Lucas closed his eyes.

She felt wonderful. Warm. Soft.

Perfect.

But what was he doing here, in her bed? He remembered returning from the hospital, anguished and exhausted. It had been late; the servants were all asleep, even Dolores. When he was a boy, she'd often waited up to see if he needed anything, though she'd never admitted to it.

Tonight, he'd been relieved to find she hadn't gone back

to those old habits, as she still sometimes did. He was too tired, too distressed to talk to anyone.

He'd gone slowly up the stairs to his rooms, pausing on the landing to look down the hall toward the guest suite. Was Alyssa still awake? Was she thinking about what had almost happened before he'd been called to the hospital?

He'd surely thought about it. Even sitting beside his grandfather's bed, the old man's icy hand in his, memories of those unplanned moments had come to him.

They had been unplanned, hadn't they? Or had Alyssa sensed it was the right time to draw him deeper into her net?

Lucas closed his eyes.

She insisted she didn't want to marry him any more than he wanted to marry her. What was the truth? He was too weary to think about it. A hot shower. A night's sleep. He'd known those were what he'd needed.

He would sort things out in the morning.

He'd gone to his suite. Undressed in the dark. Showered, let the water beat down on his neck and shoulders while he stood with his head bowed and his hands flat against the glass wall of the stall.

Restored in body if not in spirit, he'd pulled on a pair of gray sweatpants and fallen into bed, but sleep had been as elusive as peace of mind.

He'd thought about Felix. It was a good sign, wasn't it, that he was conscious? The dazed expression, the silence, would pass…wouldn't they?

And, inevitably, he'd thought about Alyssa. How it had felt to hold her. How she'd returned his kisses. How close he'd come to slaking his thirst for her, a thirst that had gripped him from those first minutes in the stable at El Rancho Grande.

He'd tossed and turned until his blankets looked as if a

demented Boy Scout had tied them in giant granny knots. Disgusted, he'd finally decided to go down to the library for a book.

Instead he'd bypassed the stairs and walked down the hall.

Where the hell do you think you're going, Reyes? he'd asked himself.

The answer was simple.

He'd gone straight to the guest suite, paused outside its closed door. He listened for a sound, checked to see if light shone under the door and found neither.

Why would Alyssa be awake at this hour? And what would it matter if she were?

Just walk away, he'd told himself sternly.

Even as he thought it, he'd turned the knob, opened the door, made his way quietly through the sitting room to the bedroom.

Alyssa lay sleeping in the canopied bed, her face gently lit by starlight. By exhaustion.

His fault.

He'd put her through hell the past day. Two days. He'd lost track. And yet, even now, she was beautiful.

His heart turned over. He wanted to wake her. Tell her he was sorry for everything, that he'd gone out of his way to frighten her in the stable, that he'd forced her to come here with him because who was he kidding? He *had* forced her. He'd given her about as much choice as a mouse trapped by a posse of cats.

The only thing he wasn't sorry for was what had happened in this room a few hours ago.

He'd wanted her. She'd wanted him. Her honest passion, her fire, had damn near stolen his breath.

The lady could be gentle as a kitten, tough as a tigress. He knew little else about her but he surely knew that.

Was that why Felix had pledged him to her?

There were a dozen other women would have been logical choices. More logical, really. Europe was filled with princesses and countesses whose families would have jumped at the chance to add Lucas's impeccable list of titles to theirs.

You could broaden the field, too. The Americas were home to heiresses whose fathers were eager for titles that would give old-world luster to their fortunes.

He'd met many of those women. American, European… they were all pretty and prettily spoiled, and every last one of them knew how to smile and flirt and please a man.

Tired as he was, Lucas had smiled.

Alyssa didn't seem to know how to do either. She was too strong, too independent. He couldn't think of another woman who'd have stood up to him the way she did.

Was that what Felix had thought would entice him? Her strength? Her independence?

Her virginity?

Felix had mentioned it but Lucas didn't believe it. Virgins were about as common as hen's teeth. Besides, virginity was overrated.

He wasn't from the old school. If men weren't held to standards of innocence, why should women be?

And, Lucas had suddenly asked himself, what in hell was he doing here, an intruder in Alyssa's bedroom? It was just that he was so damned tired. His room had seemed filled with shadows but this one—

This one seemed filled with Lyssa.

That was when he'd whispered her name. She'd awakened instantly and it was only then he'd realized she might scream or, at least, tell him to get the hell out…

Instead she'd asked about Felix in a soft, caring voice.

And when she opened her arms, it had seemed the most natural thing in the world to lie down beside her, gather her close, hold her to his heart and let her bring him the blessed comfort of sleep.

Lucas shifted his weight.

But he was awake now. Wide-awake, as far from sleep as a man could be, and he was incredibly aware of the woman in the bed with him, warm and sweet-smelling and all but sleeping on top of him.

He felt the stirrings of desire.

Bastard that he was, what he wanted from her now had nothing to do with comfort. In a heartbeat, he had an erection so hard and full it was almost painful.

How simple it would be to ease that discomfort.

A soft kiss, while she slept. A purposeful caress. By the time she was completely awake, he'd be inside her…

Madre de Dios. What kind of man would even contemplate such a thing?

Carefully Lucas slid his arm from beneath her shoulders.

"Lucas?"

Her whisper stilled him but the swift hiss of her breath as she realized how intimately they were entwined only gave him more reason to want her.

"Lucas. How did we… What are you…?"

He rolled over, lay next to her with his head raised just enough so he could see her face.

"It's all right, *amada,*" he said softly. "We took a *siesta.* Nothing more."

He could see her trying to reconstruct what had led to this just as he had done a few minutes ago. Finally she nodded.

"I remember."

"*Gracias,* Lyssa."

"For what?"

Gently he ran the tip of his index finger over her soft mouth.

"For giving me these hours of sleep. I don't know why but I could not have had them on my own."

"I understand."

"Do you?"

"When Aloysius was—when he was very sick, there were times I was so tired I could hardly hold my head up. Still, I'd get into bed and lie there, wide-awake." She took a breath, then let it out in a soft sigh that flowed over his fingers like silk. "I didn't love him the way you love your grandfather but it's hard to watch when someone who's been part of your life is suffering."

Lucas smiled. "Does my love for Felix show?"

"Like a badge of honor." She smiled, too. "He must love you the same way."

Lucas's smile tilted. "Amazing," he said softly, "but I have never before lain with a woman and discussed my feelings for my grandfather."

Color rose to her face. "You haven't exactly lain with me, Lucas."

"No." His voice grew husky. "I have not." His gaze dropped to her mouth, then lifted to her eyes. "All the more reason for me to leave your bed, *amada.* But first, a kiss good night."

Her breathing quickened. "I don't think that's—"

"One kiss," he whispered, and took her mouth. Gently. No force. No coercion. If she tried to stop him, he would stop.

He would die…but he would stop.

But she didn't stop him.

Instead the sound she made against his lips was so delicate it made his heart pound.

"Lucas," she said against his mouth. "Lucas…"

He answered by cupping her face with his hands.

She answered by parting her lips to his.

The taste of her made his head swim. She was honey. She was the richest Spanish sherry made from the ripest fruit, sweet and warm from the sun.

Her hands rose. Threaded into his hair. He groaned and slipped his tongue between her lips, felt her momentary hesitation and then she made another of those little sounds that drove him half out of his mind and sucked delicately on the tip.

A rush of heat sizzled through his body.

Leave her bed now, Lucas.

He could hear the voice inside him, hear its tone of command but he could no more obey that order than he could stop the tide of desire rising within him.

He couldn't leave her. She didn't *want* him to leave her. Not if she was looping her arms around his neck and drawing him even closer.

So close that he stopped thinking.

Touch. Taste. Smell. Sound. Those were the only things that mattered. The taste of her skin, there. Right there, in the hollow of her throat. At the juncture of throat and shoulder. At the elegant angle of her collarbone…

Alyssa trembled in his arms.

"Lucas," she whispered, "ohmygod, Lucas…"

"Yes," he said, *"si, amada."*

He whispered to her. In English. In Spanish. Words of need. Of desire. Words that made her gasp with shock.

With pleasure.

"Amada. Let me. Let me—"

"Yes," she said, "please, yes," when she felt his hands at the sash of her robe but his fingers were uncharacteristically clumsy and an eternity seemed to drag by until he finally fumbled the knot open.

The halves of the robe fell apart, revealing her to him.

Alyssa, his Lyssa, was more than beautiful. She was exquisite, everything he'd ever imagined, everything he'd ever dreamed.

And so feminine, so delicate, it made his heart leap.

He bent his head to worship her.

He cupped one rounded breast. Brought it to his mouth. Kissed the silken slope, then touched his finger to the softly pink nipple and she cried out in shock.

He knew what she was feeling because he felt it, too. The excitement. The hunger. He'd felt it before, the hot demand of sexual craving, but never like this.

Never like this.

He looked at her face. Her eyes were clouded, unseeing with passion.

Slowly he drew the nipple into his mouth, sucking, gently biting, laving her flesh. A cry broke from her throat, so wild and raw that he groaned.

He kissed his way down her torso, touched the tip of his tongue to her navel, kissed her belly and finally reached the soft curls that guarded her feminine delta.

She dug her hands into his hair.

"No," she said brokenly, "Lucas, you can't—"

He caught her wrists, brought her hands to her sides. Nuzzled against the dark curls, found her center and kissed her.

She cried out again and arched against him.

"Lyssa," he said hoarsely, and he let go of her wrists, slipped his hands beneath her and lifted her to him. Her hands were in his hair again but, this time, she wasn't trying to stop him.

She held him to her, sobbing as he put his mouth to her, found that sweetest of flowers and kissed it, sucked on it, nipped it until she screamed into the night, a scream of release, of the ultimate completion.

He could feel her orgasm rip through her body, feel it consume her and as it did, he sat back, tugged down his sweats, kicked them off and came back to her.

"Lyssa," he said.

Her eyes cleared and he felt his heart expand when she looked up at him.

"Lyssa," he said again, *"amada..."*

He held her gaze as he parted her thighs. As he guided his rigid length to her.

"Lucas," she whispered.

Later he would play that one word over and over in his head and hear in it what his fevered brain had not been willing to let him hear this first time.

He bent to her and kissed her mouth and, as he did, he entered her, sank into her, groaned as she sobbed his name against his lips.

She rose to meet him, her hands around his biceps, her fingers digging into his muscles as her silken heat closed around him.

"Lyssa," he said, "oh God, Lyssa..."

And then he stopped moving. Damned near stopped breathing.

Alyssa was a virgin.

For a heartbeat, he held still above her, his life, his breath seeming to hang suspended on the brink of eternity.

"Yes," she said, "please, yes."

Slowly, so slowly he thought it might kill him with pleasure, he sank into her. Her eyes closed. His name sighed from her mouth.

He could feel his own release rushing toward him. He wasn't ready for it. Physically, yes, but in every other way he wanted this moment to go on and on.

He was poised on the very edge of a cliff with all the world spread out beneath him. It would take a god to stay still.

But he was only human. And when Alyssa moved, when her body arched, when her womb began tightening around him, Lucas knew he was lost.

She sobbed his name. She reached her hand to him. He caught it, caught the other hand as well, brought them to his mouth, then entwined his fingers with hers against the cool ivory sheets.

"Lucas," she said again.

Her voice broke. She was afraid, he thought in wonder, and he bent and kissed her mouth.

"I'm here, *amada,*" he said thickly. "I'll be with you this time. Just let go and fly with me. Fly with me…"

Alyssa sobbed his name. Lucas flung back his head. And, just as he had promised, they flew together into the inky blackness of the endless night.

CHAPTER NINE

WAS this really what it meant, to lie with a man?

Alyssa tightened her arms around Lucas, stunned by the transcendent passion of his lovemaking.

I'll be with you this time, he'd whispered, and he'd kept his promise. The power of his climax had driven her higher, higher, higher…

Was this what sex was? Pure, white-hot magic?

Yes, she was a virgin but even virgins knew something about sex. That girls whispered about it and giggled. That some women rolled their eyes and said, in bored voices, it wasn't all what it was supposed to be.

Alyssa had never had anyone she could ask. In private school, the girls moved in tight little cliques and she, shy and leggy and more comfortable around horses than people, was always on the outside looking in. By college, it was too late to ask. Feeling naive was bad enough. She didn't want to feel stupid, too.

Once, right after her first period, she'd started to ask questions of her mother. Elena Montero McDonough had blushed, waved her hand at the horses that ran on the ranch back then and said Alyssa had all of nature for a classroom.

Maybe. But a stallion mounting a mare had nothing to do with what had happened in this bed.

Sex, it turned out, was not all about the stallion's domination and the mare's submission.

It was about giving yourself to a man. The feel of his body possessing yours. The heat of his kiss. The touch of his hand, the knowledge that he could make you want him, want him, want him…

Want the enemy. Want a stranger.

Alyssa's throat constricted. She wanted to weep, not for what she had done but for what it should have meant. What it *had* meant, those wondrous transcendent moments as Lucas made love to her.

Except it hadn't been love. It had been lust. Calculated lust, for all she knew. It was the stallion and the mare all over again.

The mare Lucas had crossed the ocean to buy.

How could she have forgotten that?

"Lyssa?"

His voice was husky. He was still lying on top of her, his weight bearing her down into the softness of the bed. She wanted to hit him with her fists. Wanted to wrap her arms around him and tell him—tell him—

"*Amada,* are you all right?"

She swallowed dryly. He lifted his head, his hazel eyes questioning. What did he think she would say? That what had just happened changed everything? That she would do whatever he wanted? Go home, accept that nothing she could do would save her mother's land?

The truth was, she had no idea what he wanted her to do…

Except bend to his will.

In the short time she'd known the Spanish prince, she had lost everything to him. Her home. Her future and now, her virginity. The only thing she had left was her pride, and she would never let him take that.

"Would you get off me, please? You're heavy."

He blinked. Apparently he was accustomed to a different kind of pillow talk. She was probably supposed to be telling him how wonderful he was, how exciting…

He was. He was all that and more.

"Sorry. I didn't realize…" He rolled off her. Her body was damp; the air felt cold on her flesh. The robe lay crushed beneath her and she grabbed the edges of it and pulled them together.

Lucas leaned over her.

"Are you okay?"

"I'm fine."

"I didn't realize…" He cleared his throat. "I didn't think you were—"

"Really?" She sat up, her back to him. "But that was part of the deal, wasn't it? Aloysius's assurance to Felix that I was a virgin?"

He put his hand on her shoulder. "*Amada.* I'm sorry you're upset. I didn't…I didn't mean for this to happen."

His voice was low. Husky with remorse. Somehow, that made it worse.

"Didn't you?"

The clasp of his fingers tightened. "What is that supposed to mean?"

Alyssa shrugged off his hand, stood up and knotted the sash of the robe at her waist.

"I've been around horses all my life."

The bed creaked. She heard the pad of Lucas's feet and then he was standing in front of her, his eyes narrowed.

"And?"

There was warning in the single word but she didn't

care. The only warning that mattered was one that would have kept her from surrendering to him half an hour ago.

"And," she said, wishing she were wearing more than this thin robe, wishing he weren't so flagrantly, magnificently naked, "and I know all those theories about the best ways to make a mare submit to a stallion."

Silence filled the room. Then Lucas reached for his sweatpants and stepped into them. His voice, when he spoke, was frigid.

"You think I seduced you to force you into some kind of obedience?"

An image of him kneeling between her thighs flashed through her mind, along with the memory of how it had felt to have him deep inside her.

"Alyssa? Is that what you think?"

Looking at him, hearing the taut anger in his words, she didn't know what to think. All she was sure of was that admitting doubt would be a sign of weakness.

"What I think," she said evenly, "is that I've made a terrible mistake."

He looked at her for a long moment, his face stony. Then he nodded.

"I agree. It was the worst possible mistake. Unfortunately we cannot undue it."

"No. We can't."

"I took your virginity."

That was what he said but the words sounded wrong, as if he meant something entirely different.

"I should have believed my grandfather when he told me you were intact."

Color flooded her face. She supposed the term was correct but it sounded cold, as if it were a description in an auction-house brochure. *The piece for sale is intact...*

"And now you've lost your bargaining chip. Deliberately, but you've lost it, nonetheless."

Alyssa blinked. "My what?"

"Ah, *chica,* it's too late for that innocent look. You know damned well what I'm talking about. Felix's values are those of another time. He saw your virginity as a requirement for your bride price." Lucas's mouth thinned. "But I don't give a damn whether a woman's a virgin or not and most certainly, I am not looking for a bride." He flashed a thin smile. "Which is why, I suppose, you felt desperate enough to toss me this morsel."

"You think that I…?" Enraged, Alyssa flew at him, hand raised, but he caught her by the wrist and twisted her arm behind her back. "You were only in this bed because I felt sorry for you, and God knows why I was that stupid! *You* were the one who turned an act of—of kindness into a— a lesson in seduction."

"Seduction?" His teeth showed in a lupine smile. "What happened in this bed is the same as what happened the day we met. You couldn't control yourself here any more than you could control that horse."

"Bastard," she hissed, "you no-good, egotistical—"

She went for his eyes with her free hand. Lucas caught it, drew it behind her where he manacled both her wrists. The action lifted her to her toes.

"Do you take me for a fool, *chica?* Nothing you do will persuade me to honor the stipulation you keep insisting you don't want me to honor."

"I'd sooner marry a—"

"So you have already said." He smiled, though his eyes remained cool. "I have known many clever women, too many to be taken in by you."

"I wouldn't doubt that for a minute," she panted as she

struggled to free herself from his grasp. "I saw one of them, remember? That—that wind-up toy with the bleached hair, big boobs and a brain the size of a walnut!"

Lucas grinned. "An excellent description, *amada*. But at least she admits she's after something when she lures a man into her bed."

"Pig!"

"Is that the best you can do?" He let go of her and strode to the door. "Tomorrow," he said grimly, "I will speak with my attorneys."

"It's today," she said, flinging the words at him. "And at least you finally said something intelligent."

"Here's something even more intelligent. I am sure they will see that the entire contract is a farce and I am liable for nothing."

"You are liable for the money you owe me!"

"My corporation owes it, and not to you. To Norton, as executor."

"Dance around all you like. Your grandfather made a deal and you're stuck with it."

His eyes flashed. "But not with you, *chica*."

"Trust me, Your Mightiness. The feeling is mutual." Alyssa glared at him. "When will you meet with your lawyers?"

Amazing, Lucas thought. She had to know she was on the losing end of the battle, that his attorneys would find a way to void the entire contract, but she was still behaving as if she were his equal.

She'd been like that in bed, too. Shy, at first. Holding back. Then, little by little, coming to life beneath his hands and mouth. Showing him what she wanted. What pleased her.

What had pleased him was the simple act of making love to her. Not that it had felt simple. He'd been with a lot of women, more women than most men, perhaps, but what had happened in this room, this bed, had seemed far more complex than anything he'd known in the past.

The act had seemed richer. Fuller. At the end, when she'd trusted him enough to let go and come with him...

When she'd done that, when she'd contracted around him even as the power of his own orgasm shot through him, he'd felt—he'd felt—

"Don't just stand there, Your Highness! I want to know when this meeting will take place! And, of course, I intend to go with you."

She intended to go with him? He almost laughed. She had no more right to attend a meeting with his lawyer than she had to keep claiming El Rancho Grande should be hers.

He looked out the window. The sky glowed pink with the morning light. No one would be in the Madrid offices of Madeira, Vasquez, Sterling and Goldberg, but that presented no problem.

The answering service would take the message. Ricardo Madeira himself would return the call within minutes.

There were occasional benefits to being Prince Lucas Reyes, even if this woman chose not to see them.

And having Alyssa with him might be an advantage. Let Madeira see precisely what he was up against.

"Be downstairs in one hour," he said brusquely. "And be prompt, *amada*. I do not like to be kept waiting."

Could an enraged woman pass up such an opportunity? He had taken all the time in the world to make love to her and she knew it, but she had the feeling she was losing their verbal war. Here was a chance to make points.

"Yes," Alyssa said sweetly, "I know how quickly you like to do things."

She knew instantly she had pushed him too far. His eyes

went from gold to green; the bones in his face stood out in harsh relief.

"Really," he said, very softly.

She stumbled back. "No," she said, the one word a terrified breath.

It didn't matter.

Lucas grabbed her. Drew her to him despite her struggles and caught her face with one hand.

"Watch what you say, *amada*. Or I may have to take you to bed again and make love to you until you beg me for release."

"In your dreams!"

He laughed softly. "No, *amada*. In yours."

He lowered his head and kissed her hard. Deep. Kissed her with a passion that bordered on cruelty. Then he flung her from him.

"An hour," he said coldly. "Or I leave without you."

The door slammed shut behind her. Alyssa didn't move. Then, after a long moment, she touched the tip of her tongue to her lips, tasted Lucas, his heat, his possession...

And closed her eyes in despair.

There were tiny spots of blood on her thighs.

On the sheets.

The blood on her thighs was easy to deal with. A hot shower, plenty of soap and the blood drops were gone even if the pain in her heart was still there.

The sheets were different. She agonized over what to do with them. The thought of one of the maids seeing that blood and knowing what had happened was more than she could bear.

Quickly she stripped the bed, carried the sheets into the

bathroom, sponged them clean, then dried them with the built-in hair dryer.

She dressed in the same clothes she'd been wearing since the evening Lucas had taken her from the ranch, whenever that was. One day. Two days. Three. She'd lost track.

One of the maids had been thoughtful enough to wash and press the garments. They looked like hell but they were, at least, clean. Not that she gave a damn. Who cared how she looked? She certainly didn't.

She left her room fifteen minutes before the hour after giving the timing some thought. Instinct told her to saunter down the stairs a few minutes late. That same instinct warned that if she were late, Lucas would leave without her.

Being early, waiting for him so that he'd seem to be the one who was late, seemed the best solution.

No such luck.

He was already in the vast entry foyer, lounging carelessly in an elaborate leather and wood chair that reminded her of a throne. Deliberate on his part, no doubt, she thought coldly.

He rose when he saw her and she knew she'd lied to herself about not caring how she looked. Lucas looked—why not admit it? He looked magnificent. His dark blue suit had surely been custom-made to suit his broad shoulders, narrow waist and long legs. Beneath it, he wore a crisp white shirt and maroon tie. She could tell he'd just showered: drops of water glittered like tiny jewels in his midnight-black hair.

He'd shaved, too. The dark stubble that had covered his jaw was gone.

The dark, sexy stubble that had felt so delicious against her thighs, her breasts…

"You need new clothes."

Alyssa drew herself up. "I need nothing from you, Your Mightiness."

A dangerous glint flared in his eyes. "Clothes, and manners. We are about to meet with Ricardo Madeira. You will not address me with disrespect, nor will you argue with what I say."

"I also will not curtsy," she informed him as they stepped into the back of the long black Rolls-Royce waiting in the driveway. "I suggest you keep that in mind."

To her surprise, he laughed. "I think I would have known you had Spanish blood even if no one had told me your middle name was Montero."

"I hate to disappoint you, but my blood is pure Texan. The Montero name dates back four centuries in the New World. I am descended from conquistadores."

Another quick laugh. "Some would say that is nothing to boast about."

"They did as men did in those times. And they were brave and fearless."

"What of your real father? Montero? Did he divorce your mother?"

"He died, when I was two."

"So you don't remember him?"

She shook her head. It was one of the sorrows of her life that she had no memory of the father who had surely loved her as Aloysius never had.

"No. I don't."

"When did McDonough adopt you?"

"When my mother married him. I was four."

Why was she telling him all this? She never talked about her past to anyone. Losing the father who'd loved you to be raised by one who didn't was no one's affair but her own.

"He was unkind to you?"

"I don't see that any of this is your concern."

"I have no idea what is or is not my concern until I've talked with Madeira."

"Until *we've* talked with him. This situation is intolerable. It must end."

Intolerable, Lucas thought. Being with him. Making love with him. Learning she was betrothed to him. Intolerable, all of it.

She was right. Of course, she was right...

Frowning, he leaned forward.

"There's no traffic," he told Paolo sharply. "Surely we can go faster."

The road wound through lush green countryside dotted with elegant villas and, tucked back among stands of orange and encina trees, enormous mansions.

Signs flashed by. Marbella was just ahead.

That explained the scent of the sea. Alyssa had never been to Spain but she knew Marbella was in the south, on the Mediterranean, facing across a narrow strip of it to North Africa and the mysteries of Tangiers.

She knew this was the gold coast, the home and playground of fabulously rich Spaniards and Europeans. Horses were expensive to breed and raise, the Andalusians of the quality the Reyes name was known for took "expensive" up another notch, and the cost of the Reyes acreage would be extraordinary.

Of course, the prince could afford it. He had no heart but he had money, power and arrogance enough for a thousand men.

"Most Andalusian breeders ranch further inland but I prefer the La Concha foothills." Lucas gave her a level look when she turned toward him. "That's what you were wondering, wasn't it? Why I breed horses here?"

"Why should I think about your horses at all?"

"Because you claim to be a horsewoman."

"I *am* a horsewoman, *señor.*"

"Most certainly." His words dripped sarcasm. "I could tell that by the way you handled that black monster."

"Bebé has fine bloodlines. And he was not at fault!"

"Bebé has the bloodlines of brontosaurs but you're right, he was not at fault. You were."

"That shows how little you know about me."

Lucas smiled coolly. "I know more about you than most men, don't I, *chica?*"

Alyssa turned crimson. "I was wrong when I called you a pig. They're actually intelligent creatures with bad press. Exactly the opposite of you."

Hell. He couldn't blame her for taking offense but, damn it, he was still angry. If only he could clear his head of the image of her, naked in his arms. Naked, and trembling, and pleading for his possession…then telling him, in a voice that would have frozen tap water, to get off her.

The time to have done that was when he realized she was a virgin but he was a man, not a saint. So he'd taken what she had offered.

Afterward, lying with her still in his arms, he'd felt a tenderness that was new to him, and a hunger to make love to her again.

First, though, he'd wanted to tend to her. Gently, with a warm, damp cloth. He'd wash her, kiss away any soreness.

Instead she'd insulted him. Made it clear what had happened had meant nothing to her. That had infuriated him, and he'd responded in kind. Which was just as well, he thought as the Rolls-Royce slowed, then stopped in a square lined with white stucco villas and palm trees.

It had sent him to the phone to make this appointment.

Paolo opened the door. Lucas stepped out and offered his hand to Alyssa, who ignored him.

"I thought your attorneys were in Madrid."

"They are. Madeira would have flown down here, of course—"

"Of course," she said with a scathing smile.

"But, as luck would have it, he's in Marbella this weekend. He's meeting us in a friend's office. Well? Are you getting out of the car, or are you going to stay here and sulk?"

Alyssa tossed her head, brushed his hand away and stepped into the cobblestone courtyard.

Good, Lucas thought viciously. She was making it easy to forget any sentimental claptrap about what he'd felt in bed with her. Amazing, the spin even a sensible man could put on taking a woman's virginity.

Madeira would review the contract. He'd agree that whole damnable stipulation was illegal, admit he had added it only because Felix had insisted. Lucas would pay the balance of what Reyes owed to Thaddeus Norton, the McDonough executor.

Then, as new owner of the ranch he didn't want, he'd commit an act of charity and sign it over to Alyssa Montero McDonough, who would then get the hell out of his life.

He supposed he could have done all this without consulting his attorney but this would make striking out the marriage clause legal and official. If Felix recovered... No. When Felix recovered, it might upset him but Lucas would deal with that when it happened.

Right now, the important thing was voiding that damned stipulation without leaving any loose ends behind.

So simple. It was almost enough to make him smile.

* * *

It was a good thing he hadn't actually gone ahead and smiled, Lucas thought two hours later.

Madeira expressed his sorrow at Felix's illness. Lucas thanked him. Madeira offered coffee. Lucas brushed it aside and handed the attorney the copy of the contract Thaddeus Norton had given him.

Madeira didn't bother looking at it.

"I had your grandfather's files faxed to me, Prince Lucas, the moment you phoned."

"Good, because I don't want to waste time. I want your legal opinion on this as quickly as possible." Lucas smiled knowingly. "Of course, I already know it's not legal. Parts of it, at any rate…but then, you must know that, too, since you wrote it."

Madeira smiled politely. "I am not in the habit of writing illegal contracts for my clients, Your Highness. If you will just give me a minute…"

An hour passed. Lucas glowered while the attorney read. Hummed. Tapped his pencil against his nose. Made notes.

Finally Madeira looked up.

"Not illegal," he said. "Unenforceable."

"The same thing," Lucas snapped.

The lawyer sat back, crossed one leg over the other, steepled his hands under his dew-lapped chin and smiled.

"Not at all, sir. The contract lays out terms agreed upon by your grandfather and Aloysius McDonough. Legal? Absolutely. Unenforceable? *Si.* I apprised Felix of that fact at the time."

Lucas felt a muscle flicker in his jaw.

"What," he said carefully, "does that double-talk mean?"

"It means, Your Highness, that this is well-crafted document."

The muscle in Lucas's jaw flickered again. "Undoubtedly, but as we have already agreed, you wrote it."

"Yes. But your grandfather had a hand in drafting some of the more unusual clauses."

"Let's get to the point." The men looked at Alyssa. Of course, she thought coldly. They had all but forgotten she was there. "You said this thing isn't illegal but it is. Selling women into slavery has actually been illegal for centuries." She paused for emphasis. "In my part of the world, anyway."

"No one sold you into anything," Lucas said sharply.

The attorney nodded. "Certainly not."

"Ms. McDonough is right, Madeira. Let's get to the point. I own El Rancho Grande."

"No."

"Well, of course, I meant I will own it should I choose to pay the balance of the selling price."

"And marry the lovely *señorita.*"

"That's ridiculous!"

Lucas and Alyssa spoke with one voice. Madeira folded his hands over his little belly and sighed.

"That's exactly what I tried to tell your grandfather."

"Well, then? What's the problem?"

"The problem is that legally, a contract is a contract. It's the meeting of the minds that's important."

"More double-talk," Lucas snapped.

Madeira shook his head. "What I'm saying, Your Highness, is that enforceable or not, contracts of this sort stand as written unless voided by the signatories." The lawyer peered at Alyssa. "One of those parties is deceased." He looked at Lucas. "And the other is incapacitated." His expression turned solemn. "Did I tell you how sorry we were to hear about your grandfather?"

"You did, yes." Lucas cleared his throat. "So, what are

you telling me, Madeira? That there might be reasons an un-enforceable contract *can* be enforced?" He flashed a chilly smile. "That's a bit too much bullshit even for a lawyer."

"Let me ask you something, Prince Lucas. Your grandfather and I discussed his giving you his power of attorney but there doesn't appear to be any such paperwork in his file."

"What does it matter? I represent the Reyes Corporation, not my grandfather."

"Ah, but Prince Felix signed this agreement in his own name, not that of the corporation." Madeira paused. "Of course, you can simply renege on the contract."

"Not pay the balance of the money?"

Alyssa made a muffled sound. Both men looked at her.

"Without that money," she said carefully, "the bank will take the ranch."

"Unfortunately," the lawyer said, "that is not Prince Lucas's problem."

"No," Lucas said coldly, "it is not."

Alyssa rose to her feet. "Despite everything, I know there's a decent human being somewhere inside you."

The lawyer blanched. "Señorita McDonough!"

"I know that because I know you love your grandfather. Surely there must be a way—"

"For you to get my money and my title? Sorry, *amada.* There isn't. Nice try, though."

Alyssa looked at him for a long minute. Her eyes glittered; was it with anger or frustration or maybe even despair?

Without another word, she stalked from the office.

Lucas watched her go. Then he cursed, shot from his chair and went after her.

CHAPTER TEN

LUCAS ran down the steps, out the door and into the courtyard.

There was no sign of Alyssa, which was impossible. How could a woman vanish in the blink of an eye?

"Sir?"

She'd had, what, a second's lead? Not even that. He'd been right on her heels.

"Prince Lucas! Your Highness!"

His driver hissed the words but they carried easily on the warm, still air. A woman walking an obese poodle stopped and stared as Paolo, gesticulating wildly, hurried up to Lucas.

"I called out to Ms. McDonough, sir, but she went right past me."

"Are you Prince Lucas?" the woman with the fat poodle said. "Oh, you are! Can I have your autograph?"

"Where?"

"Anywhere! On my hand. No, my shirt. No, on Frou Frou's collar—"

"Where did she go?" Lucas demanded, turning his back to the woman and the poodle.

"That way, sir. She went toward the corner."

"Oh my," the woman said. "This is so exciting!"

Lucas shot the woman and dog a look that silenced her and started the little dog yapping. Wonderful, he thought coldly. Soon, all of Marbella would know a woman had run from the Prince of Andalusia.

Well, let Alyssa run. He'd be damned if he'd make a fool of himself by chasing after her. No way would he—no way would he—

"*Mierda,*" he snarled, and set off running.

He saw her as soon as he turned the corner.

At this hour on a weekend morning, the streets were already busy. Tourists were window-shopping; people were searching for just the right table at just the right *café al aire libre.*

Still, Alyssa stood out in the crowd.

Everyone was strolling but she was moving fast. Added to that, she was the only woman on this expensive stretch of real estate wearing a leather jacket, black trousers and boots. Shorts, navel-skimming T-shirts, bright summer dresses and sandals were the order of the day.

She really did need new clothes, Lucas thought, and grimaced at the irrelevancy of the idea. She was running away from him. What did he care about her clothes?

He slowed to a brisk walk. He'd drawn enough curious glances. Better to move at a slightly faster pace than she. He'd catch up to her in a minute or two.

A workable plan, except Alyssa picked that moment to look back. Their eyes met; she spun away and began to run.

"Damn it," Lucas growled.

He shouted her name. It didn't stop her but it drew the attention of other people. *Dios,* he was the new spectator sport of Marbella.

"Alyssa!" he yelled again.

Then he cursed and took off after her.

His stride was much longer than hers; it gave him a distinct advantage. Within seconds, he was only a couple of feet behind her. By the time they reached an intersection, he was only an arm's length away.

And then, everything blurred.

Alyssa stepped off the curb.

A horn blared. A red truck was barreling down the road toward her. Lucas shouted her name and leaped off the curb.

He hit her, hard. They fell, rolled and the truck shot by them, horn still blaring, so close he could smell the rubber of its skidding tires and feel the dust from the cobblestones blow into his face.

For an instant, the world stood still. Lucas could hear nothing but its hush and the drumbeat of his heart.

"Alyssa," he whispered, and she turned in his arms and sobbed his name.

He shut his eyes. Gathered her to him. *"Amada,"* he said thickly. *"Madre de Dios, amada!"*

The truck had stopped. The driver ran back and squatted beside them. "Are you okay?"

Lucas nodded. He cupped Alyssa's head, brought her face to the crook of his neck.

"The lady just stepped out in front of me. I couldn't—"

"Si. I know. It was not your fault."

"You want an ambulance? A doctor?"

"No," Alyssa whispered, her tears hot on Lucas's throat. "Please. No ambulance. No doctor."

Lucas nodded again. It seemed all he was capable of doing. "We're fine," he said.

Then he rose to his feet with Alyssa in his arms. A crowd had gathered; he ignored it. The only thing that mattered was his Lyssa. She was safe and he had her back. What could be more important?

The Rolls-Royce came to a stop beside them. Paolo, white-faced, peered out the window.

"Sir. I—I followed you with the car. I don't know if that was what you wanted but—"

"Paolo," Lucas said softly, "you just doubled your pay."

Gently he put Alyssa into the wide back seat, then climbed in after her.

"Take us home, Paolo."

When he reached for Alyssa, she went straight into his arms.

He carried her into the house, just as he had only a day ago.

Then, she'd been rigid in his embrace. Now, her arms were looped around his neck. Her face was buried against his chest, and Lucas thought of how wonderful it would be to hold her like this forever.

Dolores threw up her hands and let fly a stream of saints' names when she saw them. Lucas could hardly blame her. His trousers were torn; so were Alyssa's. He could see the long, bloody scrape on her knee. Her jacket was ripped as was her blouse, and a bruise was already forming on her forehead.

"*Señor!* Oh, what has happened? The poor lady—"

"Phone for the doctor, please, Dolores."

"No! Lucas, I don't need—"

Lucas stopped the whispered protest with a kiss. "For my sake, *amada, si?* I need to hear the *médico* say that you are all right."

While Dolores hurried to make the call, Lucas carried Alyssa up the stairs, to his rooms, and placed her carefully in the center of an enormous canopied bed. He kissed her again before disappearing inside the master bathroom and emerged a moment later carrying a small basin of warm water, a soft cloth and a linen hand towel.

"Can you sit up, *amada?*"

"Lucas. I can do this for myself."

"Of course you can. I know that. You are a strong, brave woman. You can do anything you set your mind to." Gently he lifted her against the pillows. Then he dampened the cloth and cleaned the smudges and dirt from her face with a gentleness belied by his big, powerful hands. "But I want to do this, *si?*" His tone, still gentle, assumed an edge of authority. "And you will let me. Now, close your eyes. Good. There is a tiny cut right here…"

Alyssa gave herself up to the touch of her Spanish prince. How predictable he was! First he seemed to ask her permission. Then he made it clear he would do exactly as he wanted no matter what she said.

His fingers skimmed over her face as delicately as the whisper of butterfly wings.

How arrogant her prince was.

How wonderful.

She had thought him ruled by ego but she was wrong. In a world of "me-firsters," Lucas believed in putting the needs of others before his own. His grandfather's, now hers.

Her prince was an amazing man. Complex. Generous. Exciting. If only they'd met some other way. If she could go back, undo the damned contract and meet her prince as a woman, not an obligation…

Alyssa caught her breath. Lucas's hand stilled.

"Am I hurting you, *amada?*"

She shook her head to tell him he wasn't. She didn't trust herself to speak.

When had he become *her* prince? Because that was

who he was, in her heart, and wasn't that a joke? They'd met because his grandfather and her father had come up with an arrangement that would have made the devil laugh; he'd brought her here because he was as desperate to find a way out of it as she was…

Except, she wasn't. Not anymore.

Lucas's dark head was bent over her a scrape on her hand, baring his nape. Was it only last night she'd buried her fingers in the silky hair that grew there? Kissed his throat? Sighed his name and, God, welcomed him deep, deep inside her…

"Lucas."

His name whispered from her lips. He looked up, his eyes going dark.

"Lyssa," he said softly, wrapping a hand around the back of her head, bringing her mouth to his, her breath to his…

"Your Highness? The doctor is here."

Lucas brushed his lips over Alyssa's. Then he rose to his feet, introduced her to the doctor, frowned when the doctor suggested he leave the room…and left only after Alyssa touched his hand and said she'd be fine.

The doctor poked, delicately prodded, heard the entire story—well, not the entire story but enough of it to tell her she was a very fortunate young woman. Then he prescribed a salve for her cuts and tablets to take should the rapidly-rising lump on her forehead or the cut on her knee cause undue discomfort.

"Other than that, Your Highness," he said, when Lucas rejoined them, "the *señorita* needs only a relaxing bath and a long *siesta*."

Once he was gone, Lucas shut the door, then sat down on the bed next to her.

"Does your knee hurt, *amada?*"

"It's only a little cut."

"Your head?"

"Honestly, Lucas—"

"Honestly, *amada*," he said gruffly, "you could have been killed! Is that only a little thing, too? Were you so desperate to get away from me that you would risk your life to do it?"

"No! I wasn't—" She took a long breath. "It wasn't you. It was everything. So much has happened and—and I didn't want to think about any of it anymore."

Lucas took her face in his hands. "And what happened last night?" he said softly. "Did you want to stop thinking about that, too?"

How simple it would be to say yes. To tell him last night had been a terrible mistake. She'd as much as said that this morning. All she had to do now was look into his eyes and say—and say—

"No!" The word burst from her throat on a shaky breath. "I'll always think about last night, Lucas. All of it. Your kisses. Your caresses. Your—"

He stopped her words with a kiss. "Last night was wonderful, *amada*. And then I ruined it."

"Not you. Me. I said things—"

He gathered her into his arms and kissed her again and again, until she was clinging to him.

"I accused you of things you would never do. And, *Dios,* such a gift you gave me. Your innocence…"

"You gave me a gift, too." Her cheeks colored. "I never knew—I never imagined—"

Another kiss. Then Lucas leaned his forehead against hers.

"The *médico* suggested a warm bath."

"Mmm." Lazily she stroked her hand along his jaw.

"I will run it for you."

There it was again, that mixture of tenderness and command. Alyssa smiled.

"Thank you."

"But I am not comfortable with the idea of you bathing alone, *chica.*" He took her hand from his face, turned the palm up and pressed a kiss to the tender flesh. "You are hurt."

"Really, I'm fine. You heard what the doctor said."

"The doctor did not see that truck coming at you. He did not hear the sound of its horn." Lucas drew her into his arms. "Dolores or one of the maids could stay with you."

"Honestly, Lucas—"

"There's that word again."

"Lucas. I don't want Dolores or one of the maids in the bathroom with me."

"Did you know more accidents happen in bathrooms than any other place in a house?"

She had to smile. "That's desperate."

"It's true."

"I don't care what statistics you quote me. I am not taking a bath with an audience."

"I knew you would say that, *chica.*" He held her at arm's length. "So here is what I will do. I will take a bath with you. At great personal sacrifice, of course." The low flame in his eyes made the words a lie. "How does that sound?" he added in a husky whisper.

There was only one possible answer to the question, and she gave it to him on a long, deep kiss.

He undressed her as the tub filled, cursed ripely when he saw the cut on her knee and the other scrapes and bruises on her flesh.

"I'm fine," she said lightly.

He shook his head.

"*Dios,* when I think of what might have happened—"

Alyssa touched his face. "But it didn't, thanks to you."

Lucas looked up. All at once, a fist seemed to close around his heart. He felt something, an emotion, a joy. He had no name for it. No word for it unless—unless—

"The bath," he said, shooting to his feet. "Let me check."

Alone in the bathroom, he clutched the rim of the marble sink and peered into the mirror, half-afraid he'd see the face of a stranger instead of his own.

Too many things were going on at once, that was the problem. He was worried about Felix; the foolish, impossible contract was not yet dealt with; this accident had been a close call...

Too many things. That was all.

The black marble tub was full. He shut off the water, turned on the circulators, went back to the bedroom and lifted Alyssa in his arms, but there was no fooling her.

"Lucas?" she asked quietly. "What's the matter?"

He looked down at the face that had once belonged to a stranger and that fist around his heart gave another knowing squeeze.

"Nothing," he said. "It is just that you are so beautiful..."

He kissed her and tried to ignore the feel of her naked flesh against him. She'd been in a terrible accident. This was no time to think about making love.

But it was the right time to tend to her bruises.

He kissed her forehead. Her bruised cheek. Her mouth. She sighed with pleasure.

Slowly he put her on her feet. Then he sat on the edge of the tub, drew her forward so she stood, naked, between his parted thighs.

Was that a bruise on her breast? No. It was only a

shadow…but he kissed it just the same, kissed the soft flesh, circled the nipple with his tongue until she moaned.

"Does this hurt, *amada?*" he whispered.

"No. God, no, it feels—it feels—"

Lucas sucked the nipple into his mouth. Alyssa swayed, clasped his shoulders, murmured his name.

The bruise on her knee. That deserved his attention, too. He pressed his lips to it gently, then kissed his way up her leg, inhaling her scent, *Dios,* drunk on her scent, on the little cries she was making.

He cupped her hips. She leaned back; her thighs parted.

"That's it," he said thickly. "Open for me. Let me see if you need to be kissed here. And here. And—"

He put his mouth to her and she came instantly, her taste honeyed against his tongue, her cry filling him with her sweetness.

Lucas rose to his feet. Trembling, she fell against him. He held her close, kissed her mouth, shuddered when he felt her hands pulling at his shirt, his belt…

Together, they stripped off his clothes. They moved quickly but when he lifted her and put her into the tub, his hands were gentle.

By the time he joined her in the steamy water, sanity was returning.

She'd been injured. And he, *Dios,* he'd forgotten everything but how beautiful she was, how much he wanted her…

"Lyssa. Forgive me, *amada.* I shouldn't have—"

She moved into his embrace. Her mouth met his and clung. She lifted her hips, wrapped her legs around him and impaled herself on his rigid length.

Lucas groaned. Kissed her. Told her that he loved her kisses, her taste, her scent but most of all, most of all he loved this. Being inside her. Being part of her. Being one with her.

No. Most of all, he loved—he loved—

Alyssa convulsed around him and he stopped thinking.

After, he wrapped her in an enormous white towel. Then he brought her to his bed. She raised her arms to him, just as she had done the prior night. He came down beside her, gathered her close and feathered kisses on her eyelids.

Moments later, the sound of her breathing told him she was asleep. He was close to sleep, too. *Dios,* how incredible this was. Sleeping with her, making love with her…

His body stiffened.

Making love without a condom.

What had become of his brain? Last night and again today, no protection. He had never been so careless in his life.

Thank God he had a box of condoms in the night table drawer to use next time.

He wanted children but unlike some of his contemporaries, he wanted them *after* he was married. Wanted them born to a woman who was his wife.

His wife…

He lay there for a long time before he fell asleep.

"Rise and shine, sleepyhead."

Alyssa dug deeper into the blankets.

"Whoever you are, go away."

"Whoever I am?" the voice said indignantly.

"You want me to think you're Lucas Reyes. But the real Lucas would never be so cruel as to wake me." Alyssa stretched luxuriously, loving the feel of the Egyptian cotton sheets against her naked body. "How do I know you're him?"

Just as she'd hoped, a warm hand cupped her face. A coffee-flavored mouth claimed hers.

"Are you convinced?" a husky voice murmured.

"Mmm. Is that coffee?"

"Uh-huh. A whole pot of it's waiting for you on the balcony. Sound good?"

"One more kiss and I'll let you know."

"Behave yourself," Lucas said sternly. "Or I'll be back in that bed with you."

Alyssa laughed softly and reached for him. He caught her hands, kissed them and brought them to her sides.

"If I get into in that bed, I'll just have to send all this stuff back. I mean, I'll have to assume you don't want any of it."

"The coffee?"

"Not the coffee, sleepyhead. The other things."

Alyssa sat up, clutching the duvet and blinking the sleep from her eyes.

"What other things?"

Lucas grinned. "Ta da," he said, and stepped aside.

Her mouth dropped open. Boxes were stacked like building blocks behind him. Big ones. Small ones. Some were wrapped in glossy paper, others were tied with gold ribbon, silver ribbon, white satin ribbon...

"Lucas?"

His grin widened. "Open one, *chica*."

"But... What is all this?"

He picked up a flat white box and tossed it to her. "Why not find out?"

Alyssa pulled at the silver ribbon and gasped. The box was filled to overflowing with sexy silk panties and equally sexy matching bras.

"I didn't know what colors you'd like," he said modestly, "so I ordered them all."

"Lucas. Honestly—"

"One of your favorite words, *amada*. Honestly, you needed something to wear."

"But not all this! Lucas, really—"

Another box landed next to her. "At least take a look and tell me if you hate my taste, *chica*. As a favor, *si?*"

She flashed him a look, told herself sternly she would not be drawn in...

And undid the ribbon.

"Oh," she whispered. "Oh, Lucas!"

"Is that a good 'oh' or a bad 'oh'?"

He sounded so innocent, but the self-satisfied gleam in his eyes gave him away.

"It's a bad one," she said primly. "Why would any woman want a dress like this? A dress made of—of gossamer and moonbeams and—and, oh God, it's so beautiful..."

Lucas caught her up in his arms.

"You are what is beautiful," he said. "And I hope you will do me the honor of wearing these things, *amada,* because it will do my heart so much good."

Alyssa looped her arms around her lover's neck.

"It will do *your* heart good, hmm?"

He grinned. *"Si."*

"And if I said no, I want to wear my own clothes?"

"I would say, these are your own clothes now, *chica*— especially since I told Dolores to toss out the others."

"You tossed out my clothes without asking me?"

"Of course. What was the point in asking when I knew you would insist on keeping them?"

He was laughing and it was impossible not to laugh with him. Alyssa ran through her mental list again. Her prince was arrogant and impossible, and why did she love him anyway?

Because she did. She loved him, loved him—

"Lyssa? What is it?"

"Nothing," she said breathlessly. "Nothing. I just—I just felt a little dizzy, that's all."

His eyes darkened. "Shall I call the doctor? Is it your head? Your knee?"

It was her heart, but how did you say that to a man who wouldn't want to hear it?

"I'm fine. Truly. I'm just—I'm thrilled that you thought of giving me such beautiful things."

"Really?" he said softly. "You feel all right?"

"I feel wonderful."

Lucas cleared his throat. "In that case... I told my grandfather we would be at the hospital by six."

"Your grandfather? You spoke to him?"

"*Sí.*"

"How is he?"

"Let's put it this way. I said we would be there in a couple of hours. He said he would be watching a news show on CNN in a couple of hours and that he would expect us at six."

"Then he's better."

"He is arrogant, demanding and dictatorial."

Alyssa laughed.

"What is so amusing? Are you suggesting I am like that?" He grinned. "Okay. Maybe just a little. But yes, Felix is better. Much better, or so it would seem." He caught her hands in his. "Will you come with me and meet him, *amada?* It is important to me."

The bright day seemed to dim.

Of course it was important to him. Once they spoke with Felix Reyes, they could settle the contract issue once and for all. Lucas would be free of her and she would be free of him.

Free to go back to Texas, never to see her prince again...

"Lyssa. Damn it, something *is* wrong. Tell me what it is and I will fix it."

Alyssa looked into her lover's eyes. He was a good man. An honorable man. A powerful man. But not even Lucas Reyes, Prince of Andalusia, could fix a heart that was about to be broken.

"What's wrong," she said lightly, "is that you've only left me half an hour to dress. A woman needs more than that, Your Highness. If I'm not properly put together, whatever will you grandfather think?"

Lucas gathered her tightly against him and stroked his hand down her back.

Si, he thought, as he pressed his lips to the top of his Lyssa's head, that was an excellent question.

What would Felix think?

The old man had poked his nose where it hadn't belonged. He'd interfered in two lives…

And miraculously changed both of them, forever.

CHAPTER ELEVEN

THE last months of Aloysius's life, Alyssa had spent a lot of time in hospitals. She was prepared for what she was certain would come next. The smell of disinfectant. Harsh lighting. The brisk efficiency of the staff that kept emotions at bay.

There was none of that in the hospital in which Felix Reyes was a patient.

The corridors were bright but pleasant; the smell clean, not antiseptic. Nurses and aides smiled and greeted Lucas cordially.

Even Felix's room was homey if you ignored the machines and monitors beeping and humming on the wall beside his bed.

Felix himself was sitting up, propped by a stack of pillows. His eyes were that combination of gold and green and brown, like Lucas's. He had a neatly trimmed white mustache and beard. Dignity and authority clung to him like a royal cloak, though not enough to disguise his obvious frailty.

A smile lit his face when he saw Lucas.

"Mi hijo," he said, opening his arms.

The men embraced. The affection between them made Alyssa's throat constrict. Her mother had been reserved, and she and her father—her adoptive father—had so rarely showed warmth to each other that the times they had stood out in her memory.

The last had been the day she'd brought him home from the hospital after he'd pleaded to leave this earth under the wide sky of El Rancho Grande.

To her dismay, tears burned in the corners of her eyes. She blinked them back just as Lucas stepped away from the bed and Felix Reyes looked at her.

"And this, of course, is Alyssa."

"Your Highness."

"It is a pleasure to meet you, child."

"I'm glad to see you're feeling better."

Felix chuckled. "Very polite. Hardly anyone would realize you had avoided saying it was a pleasure to meet me, too."

Lucas's arm curled around her waist. "Grandfather," he said softly, "Alyssa's been through a great deal."

"I understand, *mi hijo*. If I were she, I would not feel kindly toward me, either."

"I mean no disrespect, sir, but—"

"But, if I were not plugged into all these infernal devices, you would look me in the eye and tell me just what you think of an old man who had the audacity to meddle in your life. That's the truth, girl, is it not?"

Alyssa took a deep breath. "I would tell you that you and Aloysius did some things you shouldn't have done."

Felix looked pointedly at how she stood, Lucas's arm tightly around her, their bodies lightly brushing.

"And yet," he said softly, "it all seems to be working out well."

"That isn't—"

"The point. I know." He grinned at Lucas. "Aloysius told me his daughter had spirit and he was right."

"Grandfather." Lucas cleared his throat. "Are you well enough to discuss this? Because if you are—"

"Aloysius also said she was pretty. He was wrong. She is beautiful."

Lucas felt Alyssa tense. He knew she couldn't be happy to be talked about as if she were not in the room.

"Sturdy, too. Good conformation. Good hips. Excellent for childbearing."

Alyssa's face turned crimson. "Grandfather," Lucas said sternly, "I will not permit you to—"

"My apologies. I simply meant it is good to see my old friend's recommendations were valid."

"Yes, grandfather, I'm sure it is, but—"

"He said the girl would make you a perfect wife, *mi hijo,* and he was correct."

Alyssa looked up at Lucas. "I think," she said carefully, "it's best if I wait outside."

"No!" His arm tightened around her. "Damn it, grandfather! What in hell are you trying to do?"

"Why, Lucas, *mi hijo,* you almost sound as if you care for the girl."

"I do care for her." Lucas's tone softened. "I care for her very much. Too much to let you embarrass her."

"Is that what I'm doing, child? What became of that spirit we just discussed?"

"We didn't discuss anything, Your Highness. So far, you've done all the talking."

"Ah. See? It's there. The spirit. My old friend, Aloysius, described you with unerring accuracy."

"Aloysius," Alyssa said tightly, "didn't know a damned thing about me!"

"He knew you were beautiful. And bright. And that you had a tendency to be stubborn."

"I am not stubborn."

Lucas coughed. "Uh, uh—I think this conversation should wait for another time."

"He also knew," Felix said, ignoring his grandson, "that you loved his land and you would do anything to restore it and keep it wild and free."

Alyssa shook off Lucas's encircling arm and moved nearer the bed. "It wasn't his land, it was my mother's!"

Felix's smile faded. "No," he said gently, "it was his."

"It was hers! Hers and my real father's. And when my real father died—"

"Alyssa. I assume you came here to learn why Aloysius did what he did. Why he sold the land to me—and why he added that stipulation. Am I correct?"

"Absolutely correct."

"Then, you came here for the truth."

"I know the truth, Prince Felix."

"No. You do not." His tone gentled. "I pleaded with Aloysius to tell you but he kept saying the time wasn't right. I think it was the only thing about which he was not courageous."

"Grandfather." Lucas hesitated. "You've been very ill. Perhaps we should leave and let you rest. We can have this talk another time."

"Who knows if there will be another time, Lucas? I have lived a long life. I am ready for whatever comes next but I don't want to move on to that remaining adventure without telling this girl, and you, what you both need to know."

Lucas moved beside Alyssa and put his arm around her again.

"Only if she wishes to hear it," he said, tilting her face to his. "*Amada?* The choice is yours. Do you want to hear more?"

Alyssa looked into her lover's eyes. Every instinct warned her that whatever came next would change her life but as long as she had Lucas with her, she was ready for anything.

"Yes. I want to hear the rest."

Lucas bent his head and kissed her. Then he smiled, touched his thumb to her lip and turned to Felix.

"What is it we need to know, Grandfather?"

Felix hesitated. Then he cleared his throat.

"What did your mother tell you about your real father, Alyssa?"

"Only that he died when I was two."

"And his name was?"

"I don't see what this…" She sighed. "Montero. Eduardo Montero."

"And yet," Felix said softly, "you are named for the man you call your adoptive father. For Aloysius McDonough."

"Named for him? Just because his name starts with the same letters as mine hardly means that I—"

"My dear child. Montero was your mother's maiden name. Aloysius was your real father."

"No! He adopted me when he married my mother."

"He and your mother were lovers. Her family was rich and traced its lineage back to the conquistadores. His was poor." Felix smiled. "He said he could trace *his* lineage back to the Irish potato famine, and the great-great-grandfather who boarded one of the coffin ships for New York."

Alyssa shook her head wildly. "This is crazy! Why would my mother have lied? Why would Aloysius?"

"Your mother was very young. When her parents learned of the affair, they told her she could never see Aloysius again." Felix paused. "Then she learned she was pregnant."

Alyssa drew a shaky breath. "Pregnant? Do you mean…with me?"

"Yes, child. Her parents forbade her to see Aloysius or tell him of the pregnancy. They said she would have to give you up when you were born but when the time came, she could not do it."

Alyssa sagged against Lucas, who drew her closer.

"She ran away with you and worked her way through the southwest as a waitress. Meanwhile, Aloysius had heard rumors of her pregnancy. He searched for her and searched for her and when he finally found her, he asked her to marry him."

"Aloysius," Alyssa whispered. "My real father?"

"By then, you were a precocious four-year-old. You'd asked about your father and your mother had told you he was dead."

"But Aloysius found us! Why didn't he tell me who he was?"

"Your mother wouldn't permit it. She said it would be too much for a child to bear, though he always thought that perhaps, just perhaps, she felt he was not really good enough to be revealed as your true father. At any rate, she would only marry him if he agreed never to tell you the truth."

"And he went along with that?"

Disbelief roughened Alyssa's voice. Felix sighed and shook his head.

"What choice did he have, child? Abandon you both— or have you in his life, even if he had to live a lie."

A sob caught in Alyssa's throat. "And all the time," she whispered, "all those years…"

"He treated you coolly because he was always afraid he would break down and tell you what he had vowed to keep secret. As for the land…he'd bought it piece by piece, worked it as best he could but there were droughts and fires, and then your mother's illness took the last money that he had."

"He should have told me," Alyssa said. Tears ran down her cheeks. "He should have told me!"

"*Sí.* I agree. But he was afraid you would hate him for living such a lie."

"But why did he sell you the ranch? He knew I loved it. He knew what it meant to me."

"He also knew you would not be able to keep it. And that pained him, that the bank would take the only legacy he could leave you, his flesh and blood daughter."

"So you offered to buy the ranch," Lucas said.

"*Sí.* It was the perfect solution. I would buy it, the money I paid would loose the bank's hold. And then, *mi hijo,* and then the two of us realized we could do more."

"That stipulation."

"Of course. I wished you to have the right wife. Aloysius wished Alyssa to have the right man, one who would cherish her and the land she loved." Felix threw out his hands. "And here was the perfect solution."

Silence settled over the room, broken only by the electronic pings of the machines. After a moment, Lucas sighed.

"The two of you thought to play God," he said quietly.

Felix nodded. "I suppose you could say that, yes."

"You suppose?" Alyssa's voice shook. "Playing God is exactly what you did, Your Highness. First Aloysius took it upon himself to keep the truth of my birth a secret. Then you toyed with two lives. If that isn't playing God—"

"Alyssa," Lucas said softly. "*Amada,* please, don't weep."

"I'm not weeping," she said, while tears rolled down her cheeks.

Lucas's heart filled. He wanted to sweep his Lyssa into

his arms and carry her away with him to a place where she would never have reason to cry or feel anything but joy. He wanted to make her smile, make her laugh, he wanted to tell her—to tell her—

"I am tired," Felix said. "That is enough for today."

"More than enough," Lucas agreed, a little coldly. He turned Alyssa to him, cupped her face in his hands and kissed her, and to hell with having an audience. "Wait for me outside, *chica.* Will you do that? I'll only be a minute, I promise."

He waited until she'd left the room. Then he went to his grandfather's side and looked down at the old man.

"Some might say you played at being the devil," he said quietly, "not God."

"Si," Felix said wryly. "Anyone can see how the two of you despise each other."

"That is not the point, Grandfather."

The old man sighed. "I know."

"You did an awful thing, adding that marriage clause."

"I know."

"You cannot force strangers to want each other."

"I know, I know, I know. What else do you want me to say?"

Lucas reached into his pocket and took out the contract signed by his grandfather and Alyssa's father.

"I want you to scrawl your signature here, at the bottom, where I have put an addendum."

"Which says?"

"Which says," Lucas said grimly, turning the document toward Felix, "you agree that the Reyes Corporation should pay the arrears and whatever's due the bank for El Ranch Grande."

"If that is what you wish, *mi hijo.*"

"And," Lucas continued, pointing to the addendum,

"that you agree that the Reyes Corporation will deed the ranch over to Alyssa McDonough."

Felix sighed. "My glasses and a pen are on the table."

"And," Lucas said, "you agree, as well, that the marriage stipulation is null and void."

"All of that is what you wish, Lucas?"

"All of that, Grandfather."

The old man held out his hand. Lucas slapped his eye glasses and his pen into the palm.

Seconds later, the signed amendment, together with the original contract, was safe in Lucas's pocket.

"You did a terrible thing, old man," Lucas said. Then he sighed, bent down and pressed a soft kiss to Felix's white hair. "But I love you all the same. Get some rest, yes? I will stop by again later."

Alyssa was waiting for him beside a pond that was home to a pair of swans.

Her back was to him. Lucas took advantage of that and slowed his steps so he could watch her.

She had taken an awful blow today, discovering she'd not only judged Aloysius wrong but that he was also her father.

She'd wept, yes. He would have, too, if such news had been dropped in his lap. But she'd maintained her composure, kept it well enough to strike back at Felix with courage and dignity.

He smiled. *Dios,* she was amazing.

Beautiful. Intelligent. Courageous. Passionate.

His smile broadened. And, though he'd be damned if he'd admit it without a fight, she could ride a horse as well as any man.

And he would never have met her, if his grandfather had not conspired to make it happen.

Lucas's smile faded.

Still, what had been done to her was wrong. To him, too, but somehow, that didn't seem important. It was his Lyssa who had suffered in all of this.

Not anymore.

Lucas slid his hand into his pocket and felt the heavy vellum on which the contract and the addendum were written. It was over now. His Lyssa would get her land, free and clear. He would add a substantial check so she could start the process of building it back to what it had been. She'd protest, of course, so he'd have to come up with some plan she'd find acceptable. That he wanted to invest in the ranch, maybe.

Something like that.

More to the point, the stipulation had been rendered invalid.

She didn't have to marry him. He didn't have to marry her. He could tell his pilot to take her back to Texas. They could put this behind them, remember it as just a brief, hot interlude.

Alyssa turned, saw him and smiled.

Was that how he'd remember it? As sex? Would he only recall his Lyssa as she'd been in his bed? Incredible was the word for that but his heart told him he would remember these days, and his Lyssa, as more than that.

She started toward him. He watched the way she walked, that proud stride that he loved. The way her hair bounced against her shoulders. The tilt of her chin, the glow of her blue eyes.

Would that glow dim, if only a little, when she said goodbye?

A thought burned its way into his brain. A crazy thought. Something he could say that would keep her here…

When she reached him, she lay her hand lightly on his arm. "Is your grandfather all right?"

"He's fine." Lucas took her hand in his and rubbed his thumb lightly over the delicate knuckles. "A little tired, that's all."

"I'm sorry."

"For what, *chica?*"

"For being so hard on him."

"You?" Lucas smiled. "You were gentle, *amada*. More so than he deserved."

"What he did—what he and Aloysius did—was wrong but they meant well. And he's so frail…"

"Trust me, *chica*. He's a tough old bird."

"He is," she said with a little smile. "I could see you in him in another fifty years." Her smile tilted. "But I was disrespectful and I shouldn't have been. You love him and he loves you. He thought he was doing the right thing or he wouldn't have done it."

"*Si*. But it does not excuse it."

"Still, I could have—"

"You could have called him a meddling old fool, but you didn't. You could have treated him to one of those right crosses you tried on me." Lucas brought her hand to his lips and kissed it. "I'd say my grandfather got off easy."

"Honestly?"

"*Si*. And he knows it. So don't feel guilty. If anything, he respects you all the more for standing up to him."

She let out a long breath. "I feel better."

"Good." He slid his arm around her waist. How right it felt there, he thought, and pressed a kiss into her hair. "So, *amada*. What would you say to a drink at a little café with a view of the sea?"

"I'd say yes," she said, tilting her head back and smiling at him.

"And then dinner. Paella, in a little inn about an hour from here."

"Is there a fireplace?"

He grinned. "Absolutely." He drew her closer. "And, after, a drive to Monroy. It's a small town where—"

"—where some of the finest Andalusians are bred. I know about it. The first Andalusians sent to America were from Monroy."

"*Si.* That's right. I have a ranch there, too. I want you to see it." His arm tightened around her as they began walking. "It's my favorite place in all the world." He looked down, saw her give a quick little laugh. "What?"

"Nothing. Everything. It's just—I feel as if I've known you forever, and then something comes up and I realize that impossible as it seems, we're still strangers."

Lucas stopped and turned her into his embrace.

"In that case," he said huskily, "we'll just have to keep exploring each other."

Color heightened her cheeks. "I love the idea of exploring you," she whispered.

Lucas bent to her and gave her a long, deep kiss. She curled her hands into his shirt. When he raised his head, she swayed within the circle of his arms.

"Are you dizzy again? The doctor's office is only a block away—"

"I'm fine, Lucas. Really." She smiled, and the sheer intimacy of her smile made him want to drag her into his arms and ravish her right here, in the secluded little park. "It's you," she said softly. "You make me dizzy."

"I like making you dizzy, *amada.*"

"Dizzy—and forgetful. I should have asked… Did you talk to your grandfather about the contract?"

Here it was. The moment they'd both waited for.

"Yes. Yes, I talked to him about it."

"And?"

And, her worries were over. The contract was null and void. She would have her ranch, the money to bring it back to life…

"Lucas? What did he say?"

That she was free. Free of debt, free of him, free to leave him…

"Lucas? For heaven's sake—"

"He said he won't change the agreement. Not any part of it."

"Then—then the ranch is gone."

The expression on her face tore at his heart.

"No. No, it isn't, *amada.* I have the solution."

"You do?"

Lucas framed her face with his hands. The words that had been in his head for the past ten minutes, maybe for all his life, tumbled from his lips. "Marry me."

She stared at him as if he'd lost his sanity. Maybe he had, or maybe he had just found it.

"What?"

"Marry me, *amada.* El Rancho Grande will be saved. And I'll deed it over to you."

"I couldn't let you do that! You don't want to ma—"

"Is marriage such an awful idea? People marry, create homes, have children, many of them with less in common than you and I."

"But—but we don't know each other."

"Of course we do. Didn't I just say how much we have in common? Ranching. Horses." His voice grew husky.

"We're incredible together in bed." His eyes narrowed. "Unless there's someone else."

"There's no one else," she said quickly, and stopped herself before she could tell him the truth, that she loved him, that there would never be anyone else but him...

"We're right for each other, *amada*. Those two meddlers knew what they were doing." He lifted her face so their eyes met. "Marry me, *chica*. Say yes."

She wanted to. Oh, she wanted to, with all her heart. But was it enough for them to have the same interests? To be good in bed? Most of all, was it enough for her to love him when what she wanted, what she longed for, was for him to love her, too?

"Lyssa." Softly, tenderly, he brushed his lips over hers. "We can make a good life together. I promise it. Say yes, *amada*. Say yes."

Alyssa rose on her toes and kissed him.

And said yes.

Who would have imagined that the interference of two men on opposite sides of the world could result in such happiness?

Lucas had honestly thought he had everything. The land he loved. The horses he bred. A far-flung corporate empire he had created. All the women a man could want.

Surely that was everything.

Dios, how wrong he'd been.

On a soft June evening, watching Alyssa as she went from table to table in the candlelit garden of the house in Monroy, chatting easily with the guests at the engagement party he'd insisted she must have, he knew how poor he had actually been.

Until now, he'd had nothing.

His Lyssa was everything.

They had been together three weeks. Three wonderful, amazing weeks. Initially he'd wondered if he had rushed her into a situation she hadn't really wanted. For instance, there was the first time he told her he had to go to Paris on business.

"Will you be gone long?" she'd said politely when what he'd wanted her to do was beg him not to leave her or, better still, ask if she could go with him.

Why not simply tell her that's what you want? a reasonable voice inside him had whispered.

But reason had little to do with pride or idiocy or whatever in hell it was that made him so mulish and finally he'd cursed himself for a fool, swept his Lyssa into his arms and said the question was not how long would *he* be gone but how long would *she* want them to spend in Paris.

Her smile had warmed his heart.

"Do you want me to go with you? I thought—I mean, I know this isn't exactly how you'd intended things to be, Lucas, and I don't want to be in your way. I don't want to, you know, change your life."

"Amada," he'd whispered. "You have already changed it. And I love—I love the result."

Then he'd carried her to their bedroom and made gentle love to her until her whispers, her caresses had driven him half out of his mind, and he'd taken her with wild abandon while she cried out his name and shattered in his arms.

His beautiful virgin had become a gifted student. She could arouse him with a smile, a touch, and he never tired of it or of her.

In Paris, he'd introduced her to all his friends. She was shy at first but not intimidated, not even when they went to a party and his former mistress arrived with her new lover, saw him and literally threw herself into his arms.

"Lucas, darling," Delia had shrieked.

"Delia," he'd said, disentangling himself and drawing Alyssa forward. "I'd like you to meet my fiancée."

Delia had turned white. Alyssa had simply smiled and held out her hand.

"I think we met once before," she'd said sweetly. "In Texas, perhaps?"

"Meow meow," he'd whispered when they were out of earshot.

"Why, Lucas," his *novia* had purred, "whatever do you mean?"

He'd pulled her close and kissed her, and the laughter in her eyes had turned to desire.

"Amada," he'd said in a husky whisper, and he'd drawn her out into the garden of his friend's home and made passionate love to her in the gazebo, the skirt of her silk gown bunched at her waist, his mouth drinking from hers, her soft cries sighing into the warmth of the night.

At the end, when she'd trembled in his arms, he'd thought something must be happening to him, that he'd never felt this way before, so happy, so complete, that having Alyssa in his life was wonderful, wonderful—

"Lucas."

Alyssa's voice brought him back to the present as she slipped her arm through his and smiled up at him.

"I've asked Dolores to wait a little before serving dessert. I thought she might object because she's timed everything so perfectly but she said it wouldn't be a problem."

Of course it wouldn't. His staff would do anything for his Lyssa. He'd fooled no one by pretending she was his *novia* when they'd first come to Spain so he'd gathered them together three weeks ago and made the formal announcement to polite applause, which he'd expected, and then cheers, which he had not. Dolores had even kissed him, something that had never, ever happened before.

"Lucas?"

"What is it, *amada?*"

"It's a wonderful engagement party. Thank you."

He smiled. "I'm glad you're enjoying it."

"A minute ago, you looked as if you were a million miles away."

"I'm right here," he said, embracing her. "Where else would I be, if not where you are?"

Alyssa laced her hands at his nape and leaned back in his arms.

"I want you to know," she said softly, "that I am very, very happy."

"As am I."

Had he actually said that? So stuffy. So formal, when what he wanted to say, wanted to tell her, was—was—

"There. It's happening again. That distant look in your eyes. What are you thinking, Your Highness?"

He smiled at her teasing. "I'm thinking about next week, *mi princesa,* when we are married," he said huskily, "and you are truly mine."

Alyssa sighed and lay her head against his chest. "It still seems so impossible. That we should have met. That we should have—that we should have come to care for each other despite the way Felix and Aloysius trapped us."

Trapped us.

The words hurt his heart as well as his conscience. More and more, it troubled him that he had not told her the truth.

Felix had voided the contract. She was free to leave him.

He had proposed marriage when he knew she couldn't

afford to say no. That was how badly he wanted her. And what he'd done was selfish. It was immoral.

It was a lie.

How could they build a life on a lie like that, and never mind that it was a lie of omission and not commission? He'd spent three weeks telling himself that and it was time to face facts.

A lie was a lie, no matter what you labeled it.

Alyssa had to know she would lose nothing if she left him. If she stayed with him, became his wife, it had to be because it was fully her choice. Why had he been such a coward, thinking the only way he could keep her was through subterfuge?

He could tell her later, when they were alone. When they were in bed, when he could take her in his arms and show her with his mouth, his hands, his body how much he wanted her. Needed her. How much he—how much he—

"Lucas, look!"

There was a little stir among the guests. Several had risen to their feet.

"It's your grandfather."

They had invited Felix, of course, though Lucas had never expected him to come. The old man had moved into a spacious apartment on the grounds of a rehabilitation center. Lucas visited him daily; Alyssa had twice gone with him and Lucas had asked Felix, in advance, not to mention the contract.

"It upsets her," he'd explained.

"Even though I abrogated it?"

"Even though," Lucas had replied, feeling as guilt-stricken as he had at the age of five, when he'd told a whopper of a lie about his governess, a box of chalk and a Velasquez that hung on the sitting room wall.

All the more reason to come clean with Alyssa, he thought with growing urgency. And she would surely forgive him. She was happy; hadn't she just said she was?

Perhaps, given the choice, she would not have agreed to marry him three weeks ago but surely she would now.

He had to tell her. Had to hear her answer. Suddenly it mattered more than anything in the world that she should want him for all the right reasons.

"Lyssa," he began, but she was already tugging him across the terrace, to the little entourage gathered around Felix's wheelchair.

"Your Highness," she said, and made a perfect curtsy.

Felix chuckled. "A lovely gesture, but you will be my granddaughter soon. Don't you think it's time you gave me a kiss and called me by my name?"

Alyssa smiled and touched her lips to his forehead. "Felix. We're happy to see you."

"And I am happy to see you, child. You will make a beautiful princess. My Lucas is a lucky man."

Alyssa reached for Lucas's hand. "I'm lucky, too," she said softly. "So lucky that I've decided to forgive you."

"Ah. That contract."

"That contract. Even that ridiculous marriage stipulation. Without it, I'd never have met Lucas."

"True. Still, I'm sure we're both glad that I—"

"Grandfather," Lucas said quickly, "let me take you to the buffet. We have that *chorizo* you like so much, and wait until you see the size of the lobsters."

"It's all right, *mi hijo*. I know you warned me not to mention the contract but your lovely *novia* is the one who brought it up and I'm glad she did. For weeks now, I've wanted to tell her how pleased I am she decided to ignore the fact that I abrogated the silly thing."

Lucas felt Alyssa's hand stiffen in his.

"Alyssa," he said quickly, "*amada,* come into the house where we can talk."

Alyssa ignored him. "You made the terms null and void?"

"Yes, of course. The first time you came to the hospital. You left, and Lucas asked me to do it."

"Lyssa," Lucas said in the desperate tones of a man who sees his life flashing before him, "Lyssa, listen to me—"

"I was glad to. By then, I knew Aloysius and I had meant well but that we'd done the wrong thing. So I agreed to abrogate the contract and let Lucas handle things on his own. You know, pay the arrears owed the bank and deed the land to you. And, of course, that invalidated that marriage stipulation but you know all this, dear child." Felix smiled. "And, to my delight, you chose to marry my grandson anyway."

For a long moment, Alyssa didn't move. Then she swung toward Lucas and he knew he would never forget what he saw in her face.

"You lied to me," she said in a shocked whisper.

"No. Yes. I mean..." Lucas shook his head. "I wanted you. That was all I could think of, that I wanted you and that without the stipulation, you might leave me."

"So you lied."

"*Amada.* It was not that simple."

"Oh, it's very simple. And very understandable. Why wouldn't you lie? That's the way people deal with me, isn't it? My mother. My father. And now you."

"Damn it, you're not listening. I wanted you to marry me."

"*You* wanted." Her voice shook. Lucas reached for her, tried to draw her into his arms, but she jerked free of his hands, her head high, her eyes glittering with tears. "*You* wanted, and that made the lie appropriate."

His eyes narrowed. "You're overreacting."

"You lied, Lucas. Everyone lies, and nobody gives a damn what effect those lies have on my life."

"All right. I made a mistake. That doesn't change the fact that you're happy with me. That you want to marry me. That we belong together."

The minutes slipped away. Then Alyssa took a steadying breath.

"Did it ever occur to you that I'm as happy as possible under the circumstances, Your Highness? That given a choice, an honest choice, I might just as well have told you to go to hell?"

"You don't mean that."

"You're the one who lies, Lucas. Not me."

Her words were like a slap in the face—but a welcome one. The land. The ranch. That was all she'd ever wanted. Maybe he'd known that, in his heart. Maybe that was why he hadn't told her the truth.

She'd wanted everything he could give her...

But not him.

When she ran for the house, he took his time. And when he finally reached their bedroom and found her already dressed in trousers, boots and a T-shirt, he looked at her and wondered why he'd thought she was the center of his life.

It made it easy to reach for the phone and arrange to send her home.

CHAPTER TWELVE

THERE were certain absolutes in life.

Not many. A man learned that early on. Still, there were a few things that never changed.

New York in August was one of them.

In those hot, sticky dog days of summer, the city turned into a different place.

The streets were still crowded but with tourists, not New Yorkers. The city's residents fled to the Hamptons or Connecticut. The ones with reason to be in town stayed indoors, where air-conditioning provided merciful relief.

Unless it stopped working, Lucas thought grimly as he pounded along the indoor track at the Eastside Club, where the AC had given up an hour ago.

That hadn't stopped him.

He'd flown into the city in early morning, met with an investment banker who'd needed reassurance his billions would be well-spent, thought about what to do next…

And had ended up here.

No particular reason for it, he told himself as he pulled the towel from around his neck and wiped the sweat from his face without ever breaking stride. It was just that he was in the States for the first time in a couple of months. No particular reason for that, either. He just hadn't had any cause to visit the U.S.A.

Now there was. He'd come over on business and, after a long meeting, a workout at the quiet, exclusive club seemed a good idea.

Lucas's jaw tightened.

Who was he trying to kid? He'd sent his second-in-command to the States three times instead of flying over himself. The pressure of work, he'd told himself, but that was just bull.

So was lifting weights and running laps when it was ninety degrees outside and probably more than that inside, unless a man had the inclination to end up in an emergency room, but it was the only way he could think of to clear his head and keep from thinking about what had happened the last time he was in the States.

Alyssa.

Why did he waste time on such nonsense? She'd left him two months ago and, except for his admittedly wounded pride, he'd forgotten all about her.

He never thought of her anymore.

Never. Never. Nev—

"Mierda," Lucas growled and swung off the track, to the locker room.

An hour later, showered, dressed in mocs, chinos and a pale blue shirt with the sleeves rolled up and the collar open, he sat in the mercifully dark, mercifully chilly confines of a local bar, an icy bottle of ale in front of him.

He felt much, much better.

Why hadn't he done this in the first place? Not only headed here but phoned Nicolo and Damian to see if, by some minor miracle, they were in the city, too.

They were. And—

"Reyes, what in hell are you doing in the outer reaches of hell in mid-August?"

Lucas rose to his feet, grinned and held his hand out to Nicolo. Prince Nicolo Barbieri, to be exact, one of the two best friends a man could ever have.

"Nicolo."

The men grinned at each other, then embraced.

"Still ugly as ever," Lucas said.

"That's just what I was thinking about you," Nicolo countered. "Man, it's great to see you. What's it been? Six months?"

"Eight," another male voice said, "but who's counting?"

Damian Aristedes—Prince Damian Aristedes—flashed a grin and grabbed his two oldest friends in a bear-hug.

"Nicolo. Lucas. How the hell are you guys?"

"Good," both men said with one voice.

The three old pals settled into the wooden booth. The bartender, who'd known them for a long time, appeared almost instantly with two more bottles of cold ale. Lucas nodded his thanks, then turned to his buddies.

"Amazing," he said, "that the three of us should be in New York at the same time."

"This time of year," Damian said, "who'd have believed it?"

"Business goes on, no matter the weather," Nicolo said.

Damian nodded. Then a sheepish smile angled across his mouth.

"Truth is," he said, "Ivy read about an exhibit at the Museum of Natural History. A butterfly room, you know, one of those things you walk through and the butterflies swoop all around you? I suggested waiting until fall but she said the baby was at just the right age, so—"

"I know what you mean," Nicolo said. "Aimee found out about a baby tiger at the Bronx Zoo. I said, great, we'll fly over when the weather cools. She said yes, but the tiger would be bigger then and so would little Nickie."

"Priorities change," Damian said softly.

Nicolo nodded. "And for the better."

The two men grinned at each other. Then Damian turned to Lucas.

"But not for our hold-out."

Lucas raised his eyebrows. "Hold-out?"

"Lucas Reyes. Our perennial bachelor-in-residence. Still haven't found the right woman, huh?"

"You mean, I still haven't been trapped. Not that you two were," he added hastily. "I just meant that marriage isn't for every man."

"That's what I thought," Nicolo said.

Damian smiled. "Same here, but I was wrong." He took a long, cool swallow of his ale. "So, Lucas. What brought you to the city?"

"Business."

"Ah. I thought maybe it was a woman."

"Why would it be a woman?"

"Just a thought."

"Business, is why I'm here."

"Yes. So you—"

"There's not a woman in the world I'd come all this distance to see."

Nicolo and Damian exchanged quick looks. Was Lucas's tone just a little grim?

Nicolo shrugged. "Of course there isn't. As Damian said, you're our perennial bach—"

"I'd never get that deeply involved."

His pals shared another glance.

"No," Damian said, "we understand that."

"I'm finalizing a deal with a banker. Very hush-hush. He wanted some verbal hand-holding. He suggested flying over to Spain." Lucas reached for his ale, saw that the bottle was empty and signaled for another. "But I said, why go to all that trouble? I can be in New York in just a few hours."

"Absolutely," Nicolo said carefully. "Far better to hold your meeting here, where you could fry an egg on the sidewalk, than to sit on the patio at Marbella enjoying a breeze from the sea."

Lucas looked up, his eyes flat. "What's that supposed to mean?"

"It's only an opinion."

"Yes, well, your opinion is way off the mark."

"Dio," Nicolo said dramatically, "you mean there is no more sea breeze at Marbella?"

Damian started to laugh, saw Lucas's face and changed the laugh to a cough.

"Very amusing, both of you." Lucas waited until the bartender put the new bottle of ale in front of him and removed the old one. "It was simpler to hold the meeting here." He paused. "And if you want to fry eggs on sidewalks, the place to do it is the southwest."

"Florida, from what I hear. I once read an article and this guy said—"

"It's so hot in Texas," Lucas said, "you could definitely fry an egg on the sidewalk."

His friends blinked. "Texas?" Nicolo said.

"If they had any sidewalks in Texas, that is."

"Hey, Austin and Dallas and a lot of other places would be pretty upset to hear you say—"

"Texas," Lucas said coldly, "is nothing but sagebrush and

rattlesnakes baking under the sun." He took a long swallow of ale, frowned and signaled to the bartender that he needed another bottle. "If I never see it again, it'll be too soon."

This time, the look Nicolo and Damian exchanged began with *What's he talking about?* and ended with *Maybe we better find out.*

"You have something personal against Texas?" Nicolo asked with caution.

"Why the hell would I?"

"Well, I don't know, it's just that you sound as if—"

"I met a woman in Texas."

Just like that, what had been gnawing at Lucas's gut all day, hell, all day every day since Alyssa left him, was right there in the open.

Nicolo looked at Damian. *Your turn,* the look said. Damian sighed, then cleared his throat.

"And?"

"And," Lucas said, nodding his thanks at the bartender when the guy delivered a new bottle of icy ale, "and, nothing. Just, I met a woman a couple of months ago. In Texas. That's all."

Damian folded his arms and glared at Nicolo, who gave an imperceptible nod.

"That's all? You met her a couple of months ago and now you hope you never see Texas again?"

"Damn right."

"Does she have a name?"

"Alyssa. Alyssa Montero McDonough. Look, forget I said anything. The lady's history. She doesn't mean a thing to me."

"Oh. Well, in that case—"

"We met because my grandfather said he wanted me to buy a horse, except it turned out what he'd wanted me to buy was a bride."

Damian opened his mouth. Nicolo kicked him in the ankle.

"Well, of course, I'm not an idiot. I wasn't about to get trapped into marriage. I told that to Alyssa. I kept right on telling it to her, even after I took her to Spain."

This time, it was Damian who kicked Nicolo.

"I ended up doing some stupid things. Incredibly stupid," he said, his voice turning husky. He looked up, jaw set, clearly ready for trouble. "And then Felix said something he shouldn't have and the lady in question showed her true colors and left."

His friends waited. Lucas drank some ale. After a couple of minutes, Nicolo took a breath, then expelled it slowly.

"She went back to Texas?"

Lucas nodded.

"And you said, good riddance."

"Of course." Lucas frowned. "Well, I thought it."

"But you never said it to her face."

"No."

More silence. Damian knew it was his turn to take a stroll on the exceedingly thin ice.

"So, is that the problem? I mean, is that why you're in this mood?"

"Mood? What mood?" Lucas demanded, and then he shrugged. "Yes. Maybe. Probably. Idiot that I was, I let her tell me off but I never—"

"You never reciprocated."

"Exactly."

Nicolo and Damian looked at each other.

"You know," Nicolo said slowly, "not that it's any of my business, but—"

"Right," Damian said. "I mean, I'm pretty sure Nicolo's going to give you the same advice I would."

"Closure," Nicolo said, and Damian nodded.

Lucas looked at them. "Closure?"

"Sure. Go to Texas. Confront the lady. Tell her what you should have told her when she walked out."

Lucas said nothing. He lifted the damp bottle and made interlocking circles on the tabletop.

"You think?"

"Of course," said Damian. "Fly to Texas, tell the lady what's on your mind. Right, Barbieri?"

Nicolo gave a quick nod. "Abso-freaking-lutely."

A muscle jumped in Lucas's jaw. "You're right. I should have thought of it myself. I need closure. I need to tell Lyssa—"

"I thought it was Alyssa," Damian said, and waited for a kick in the ankle that never came.

The muscle in Lucas's jaw twitched. "I called her Lyssa when I thought… Never mind that. Thanks for the advice, both of you."

"Yeah, well, that's what friends are for."

The three men got to their feet, shook hands, clutched shoulders, threw friendly jabs at each other's biceps. Lucas reached for his wallet and they waved him away.

"Just go," Damian said.

They watched him stride through the bar and out the door. Then Nicolo grinned.

"The poor bastard," he said softly. "He's in love!"

Damian grinned back at him. "And another one bites the dust," he said, and waved the bartender over for celebratory shots of Grey Goose.

CHAPTER THIRTEEN

ALYSSA was not in a very good mood.

Even that assessment was generous.

She was in a miserable, horrible, don't-even-talk-to-me mood, and there was no good reason for it.

Life was definitely on the upswing.

The bank and the tax collector were off her back. El Rancho Grande was hers. She'd wasted all of two minutes debating whether or not to let the Reyes deal go through and accept the deed from the Spanish prince.

Her mouth thinned as she slipped the bridle over Bebé's massive black head.

Two minutes had been too long.

Felix Reyes had agreed to buy El Rancho Grande; Aloysius had agreed to sell it. The arrangement had been legitimate enough except for the ridiculous marriage clause. There were times she still felt as if she'd been the victim of a tasteless joke but so what?

In the end, the Spanish prince had at least done one decent thing.

Damned right, he had.

The land was hers. It would always have been hers if Aloysius hadn't lied to her all her life and never mind all that nonsense Felix had spouted about Aloysius wanting the best for her.

This was the best for her. The ranch, George and Davey working it with her, the half a dozen horses she'd taken in to board and train...

Not the Spanish prince.

Never him.

Bebé snorted and tossed his head. Alyssa smiled and stroked the stallion's arched neck.

"Of course," she told him. "You're what's best for me, too."

Yes, life was definitely good and getting better, and if she could just stop thinking about the miserable, arrogant Spanish prince and all the things she should have said to him and hadn't, she'd be in a much better mood.

She certainly didn't think about him for any other reason.

"What's the matter with Alyssa?" she'd overheard Davey whisper to George the other day.

She'd heard the *thwack* of George's tobacco juice hitting the dirt and then he'd said, well, he weren't sure but mebbe it had somethin' to do with her missing the Spanish guy.

"I do not miss the Spanish guy," she'd said, stepping into view, "and don't you two have anything better to do than gossip?"

Later, she'd apologized by making apple pie for dessert because it wasn't George's fault, thinking she missed Lucas. He had no way of knowing she hated Lucas. Despised him. That she never, ever wanted to see him again...

Alyssa's throat tightened. She blinked; her eyes were suddenly damp. A cold. A damned cold coming on, that was what it was. Just what she needed, with two more horses due this afternoon.

She led Bebé into the August morning for their usual early ride before things got busy—6:00 a.m. and it was already hot. Well, that was Texas, she thought as she swung onto the stallion's back.

It was night now at the Monroy ranch. At the estate in Marbella, too. It would be warm but the breezes would be cool, one from the lush trees, the other from the sea.

And who gave a damn?

Heat or no heat, she preferred Texas.

People were honest here, if you omitted Thaddeus who had greeted her by saying he'd be happy to buy the ranch, now that it was hers, so she could make a fresh start…and hadn't bothered mentioning he'd wanted to sell it to the developer.

And you'd have to omit her mother, too. And Aloysius. They'd lied to her in the worst way imaginable, though the more time went by, the more she grudgingly admitted she understood.

Right or wrong, they'd lied because of love.

Look what *she'd* done because of love.

No. Not love. She'd never loved Lucas. She was a liar, too, when you came down to it, but a woman had to tell herself something when she gave her virginity to a cold-hearted stranger.

Bebé snorted. Alyssa did, too, and leaned over his neck.

"You're my one and only love," she whispered as they headed down the long dirt road that led away from the house.

She urged him into a trot, then a gallop and felt some of the tension drain out of her. She belonged here, on this land, riding her own horse, not playing bedmate for a man who had never even pretended he loved her. Not that she'd wanted him to…

What was that? Something big and black, shimmering with heat waves from the sun. A bull, broken loose from the neighboring ranch? A horse?

A truck. An SUV, big and black and shiny. It was

angled across the road with the damned fool driver standing beside it.

Alyssa drew back on the reins. Bebé snorted. He didn't want his morning run spoiled by an outsider and neither did—

Oh God.

Even at this distance, there was no mistaking the identity of the man. That straight, I-own-the-universe stance. The folded arms. The proud angle of his head.

The Spanish prince was back.

She thought about turning Bebé around but that would be the coward's way out. Or she could spur him into a gallop again, ride straight on by just like the first time— but the prince, arrogant fool that he was, had walked around the SUV and was standing right in front of it.

She couldn't ride past him and while riding through him seemed a rewarding idea, spending the rest of her life in jail didn't. Lucas Reyes wasn't worth such a sacrifice.

"Come on, sweetie," she whispered to the stallion, and moved him forward at a slow walk. When she reached the prince, she stopped.

"This is private property."

"No," he said politely, "it is not."

"There's only one ranch at the end of this road and you're not welcome there."

"That does not make this private property."

Bebé pawed the ground and tossed his head. Alyssa leaned forward, crooned softly in his ear and he quieted.

"You have a nice touch," the Spanish prince said.

Alyssa said nothing. Did he actually think his compliment had any meaning?

"Especially with stallions."

A flush rose in her cheeks. She thought of half a dozen rejoinders and ignored them all.

"How did you know I'd be riding this road at this hour?"

"George was most cooperative."

"George is an old fool. What do you want here, Your Highness?"

What, indeed? Lucas knew why he'd come. Closure. The problem was, seeing Alyssa, he was no longer sure of what that meant.

He'd spent most of the flight thinking of what he'd say when he confronted her, that he knew she'd never given a damn for him, that she'd only stayed with him so she could get what she wanted...and trying to work around the fact that he'd basically suggested marriage on precisely the same terms.

When he didn't respond, she eyed him coldly. "I'm not returning the deed."

"I do not want the deed."

"Then what do you want? Quickly, please. I have work to do."

"I heard. You're boarding and training horses."

"George has a big mouth."

The prince smiled. She hated that smile. So knowing. So self-righteous.

"Yes, I am boarding and training horses. Not Andalusians like yours but then, some of us are interested in more than what's written in a stud book."

It was a low blow and she knew it. The Spanish prince's horses were all magnificent; she had ridden them with him.

"You have Bebé."

"According to you, he's a tyrannosaurus."

Lucas smiled again. "A brontosaurus, but perhaps I made a hasty judgment. He's a fine animal, now that I take a second look."

"Don't patronize me!"

"I'm not patronizing you, I'm being honest. Beauty. Courage. Heart and intelligence. Those are the qualities a man—"

Lucas frowned and fell silent. Were they still talking about horses? And what had happened to the little speech in which he'd tell her what he thought of a woman who'd use a man to get what she wanted?

True, the argument was flawed. He was the one who'd suggested marriage on pragmatic terms. They cared for each other, he'd said. And, if they married, the contract terms would be met and she would get her land.

Why blame her for leaving him once she knew there no longer was a contract?

Why blame her for leaving him after finding out he'd lied?

Why blame her for anything except breaking his heart? Didn't she know he loved her? Adored her? That his life had no meaning without her?

Didn't she feel the same way?

He knew that she did. All the times they'd made love…she'd given herself to him in ways he'd never before known, ways that surely involved the heart and not just the body.

The stallion snorted impatiently. His Lyssa was impatient, too. He could see she'd had just about enough of this foolishness.

So had he.

"Goodbye, Your Highness."

Her heels touched the stallion's sides. Lucas lunged forward and grabbed the bridle.

"Get off that horse!"

She laughed. Laughed, damn it! He had not come all this distance for her to laugh at him.

"I said—"

"I heard what you said. I suggest you let go of that bridle or I'll ride straight through—"

She cried out as Lucas lifted her from the back of the stallion.

"Put me down! What do you think you're doing? Damn you, Lucas—"

"I am damned. I will be damned for all eternity and so will you if we go on lying to ourselves and each other."

"You have the nerve to talk about lying?" Alyssa flung back her hair, her cheeks bright with color, her eyes glittering. "You're the biggest liar of all."

Lucas set her on her feet. "I admit, I should have told you the truth. That the contract no longer existed, but—"

"But, you always have to get your own way. You wanted a wife and I was handy."

"You cannot really believe that."

The trouble was, she didn't. It was the one thing she'd never been able to make sense of. If Lucas Reyes had wanted a wife, he had hundreds of women to chose from—and that left her with the same question that kept her awake nights.

"Why else would you have kept the truth from me?"

Lucas drew a long breath, held it, then let it out. He was a man stalling for time and he knew it but there had to be a way to say what he had to say without giving everything away.

He had never felt as vulnerable in his life.

"You see? You can't give me any other reason because there is none. You figured, it's time to get married and here's this—this compliant female—"

Lucas grinned. "Compliant? You, *amada?*"

"Whatever. I was available and you—"

"And I," he said, forgetting that giving everything away could be dangerous, "and I," he said, cupping her face, tilting it to his, gazing deep into her eyes, "I had fallen crazy in love with you."

Her mouth opened, then shut. Amazing. He had, for once in his life, said something his Lyssa could not counter.

"Why do you look so surprised, *chica?*" His tone softened, as did the touch of his hands. "Did you never realize what was happening to me?"

God, such arrogance! "*I* should have realized what was happening to *you?*"

"I love you," he said softly. "I adore you, *amada.* Coward that I was, rather than admit it, even to myself, I clung to that damned contract, that impossible marriage stipulation to keep you in my life."

Alyssa felt her eyes filling with tears and that would never do. She would not let the prince see her cry because—because then he would know the truth, that she loved him, had never stopped loving him—

"And..." She swallowed hard. "And that's it? You love me and I'm supposed to say, that's wonderful, I forgive you for lying to me because I love you, too?"

He smiled. "Do you?"

"Forgive you?"

"Do you love me?"

Time, the world, the universe stood still. Alyssa looked up into the golden eyes of the Spanish prince, her prince, and let the love so long trapped within her heart burst free.

"Yes," she said, "oh, yes, Lucas, yes, I love you, I love you—"

He gathered her close. Her arms rose and wound around his neck. He kissed her and she kissed him and perhaps their kiss would have lasted forever...

But the stallion whinnied, stepped forward and pushed his handsome black nose against Lucas's shoulder.

Lucas laughed.

"He's jealous."

Alyssa smiled. "He has every right to be."

Lucas's arms tightened around her. "Alyssa Montero McDonough. Will you do me the honor of becoming my wife?"

The tears Alyssa had fought against spilled from her brimming eyes.

"I would be proud to be your wife, Your Highness," she said.

Lucas kissed her again. Then he mounted the black stallion, drew his *novia* up behind him, and they rode slowly into the warm beauty of the Texas morning.

Their wedding, everyone said, was a storybook affair.

The ceremony was held on the Reyes estate in Marbella, on a hilltop overlooking the sea. The bride was beautiful and wore a gown of white lace. It was new, but her lace mantilla had belonged to the groom's grandmother.

The groom was incredibly handsome in his black tux. His two best men—there had to be two, he said, and never mind anyone who said there should only be one—were almost as handsome in their tuxes. At least, that was what Alyssa said.

Their wives, Aimee and Ivy, whispered to Nicolo and Damian that they really were the handsomest men in the world.

There was dancing and champagne, lobster and filet mignon. There was a flamenco guitarist, a string quartet and a famous rock band, and when the band veered from its image long enough to play an old-fashioned waltz, Felix got up from his wheelchair and danced with the bride.

At last, the newly married couple slipped away. The groom carried his bride up the stairs to his bedroom.

It was their bedroom now.

He kissed her tenderly, whispered to her, then stepped out on the balcony, as nervous as any man about to make love to his bride for the first time.

They had slept apart for the past month. For three months now, counting the time they'd been separated. Since their reconciliation, they'd kept their intimacy to hot, deep kisses that left them both burning with desire. It had been Lucas's idea. He wanted to take his virgin bride's innocence as he wished he had that first time.

It was his special gift to her.

He had no way of knowing that Alyssa had a special gift for him, too.

When she was alone, she took off her bridal finery and drew on the hand-sewn white silk nightgown that had been Dolores's gift to her. Her face glowed with happiness.

Lucas turned when she said his name. His heart leaped when he saw his beautiful wife.

"I love you," he said. "With all my heart."

Alyssa went to him and he gathered her close and kissed her before swinging her into his arms and carrying her to their bed, the white pillows and duvet sprinkled with red rose petals.

"Lyssa," Lucas said softly.

He kissed her. Caressed her. Undressed her so slowly that, for them both, it was the sweetest agony.

When she lay naked before her husband, Alyssa took his hand.

"This is our first night together as husband and wife," she said. "But do you remember, my Spanish prince, the first time we made love?"

Lucas brushed his mouth over hers. "I will never forget it, *amada.*"

"And do you remember that we didn't use a condom?"

His eyes darkened, but only for a second. "*Si*. And even though I long to see you with my child in your womb, *amada,* if you wish me to wear one tonight—"

Alyssa laid his hand over her belly. He looked puzzled. Then he caught his breath as he felt the new, sweet roundness of her flesh.

"*Amada.* Are you—are we—"

"*Si,* my love. We're having a baby."

Lucas's eyes filled with something that felt suspiciously like tears.

"I love you," he whispered.

Then he gathered his *princesa* in his arms and kissed her, just as the sky came alive with fireworks.

0907 Gen Std HB

MILLS & BOON®
Pure reading pleasure

OCTOBER 2007 HARDBACK TITLES

ROMANCE

The Desert Sheikh's Captive Wife *Lynne Graham*	978 0 263 19700 6
His Christmas Bride *Helen Brooks*	978 0 263 19701 3
The Demetrios Bridal Bargain *Kim Lawrence*	978 0 263 19702 0
The Spanish Prince's Virgin Bride *Sandra Marton*	978 0 263 19703 7
Bought: One Island, One Bride *Susan Stephens*	978 0 263 19704 4
One Night in His Bed *Christina Hollis*	978 0 263 19705 1
The Greek Tycoon's Innocent Mistress *Kathryn Ross*	978 0 263 19706 8
The Italian's Chosen Wife *Kate Hewitt*	978 0 263 19707 5
The Millionaire Tycoon's English Rose *Lucy Gordon*	978 0 263 19708 2
Snowbound with Mr Right *Judy Christenberry*	978 0 263 19709 9
The Boss's Little Miracle *Barbara McMahon*	978 0 263 19710 5
His Christmas Angel *Michelle Douglas*	978 0 263 19711 2
Their Greek Island Reunion *Carol Grace*	978 0 263 19712 9
Win, Lose...or Wed! *Melissa McClone*	978 0 263 19713 6
Their Little Christmas Miracle *Jennifer Taylor*	978 0 263 19714 3
A Pregnant Nurse's Christmas Wish *Meredith Webber*	978 0 263 19715 0

HISTORICAL

Housemaid Heiress *Elizabeth Beacon*	978 0 263 19775 4
Marrying Captain Jack *Anne Herries*	978 0 263 19776 1
My Lord Footman *Claire Thornton*	978 0 263 19777 8

MEDICAL™

Christmas-Eve Baby *Caroline Anderson*	978 0 263 19820 1
Long-Lost Son: Brand New Family *Lilian Darcy*	978 0 263 19821 8
Twins for a Christmas Bride *Josie Metcalfe*	978 0 263 19822 5
The Doctor's Very Special Christmas *Kate Hardy*	978 0 263 19823 2

0907 Gen Std LP

Pure reading pleasure

OCTOBER 2007 LARGE PRINT TITLES

ROMANCE

The Ruthless Marriage Proposal *Miranda Lee*	978 0 263 19487 6
Bought for the Greek's Bed *Julia James*	978 0 263 19488 3
The Greek Tycoon's Virgin Mistress *Chantelle Shaw*	978 0 263 19489 0
The Sicilian's Red-Hot Revenge *Kate Walker*	978 0 263 19490 6
A Mother for the Tycoon's Child *Patricia Thayer*	978 0 263 19491 3
The Boss and His Secretary *Jessica Steele*	978 0 263 19492 0
Billionaire on her Doorstep *Ally Blake*	978 0 263 19493 7
Married by Morning *Shirley Jump*	978 0 263 19494 4

HISTORICAL

A Scoundrel of Consequence *Helen Dickson*	978 0 263 19406 7
An Innocent Courtesan *Elizabeth Beacon*	978 0 263 19407 4
The King's Champion *Catherine March*	978 0 263 19408 1

MEDICAL™

His Very Own Wife and Child *Caroline Anderson*	978 0 263 19367 1
The Consultant's New-Found Family *Kate Hardy*	978 0 263 19368 8
City Doctor, Country Bride *Abigail Gordon*	978 0 263 19369 5
The Emergency Doctor's Daughter *Lucy Clark*	978 0 263 19370 1
A Child to Care For *Dianne Drake*	978 0 263 19545 3
His Pregnant Nurse *Laura Iding*	978 0 263 19546 0

MILLS & BOON®
Pure reading pleasure

NOVEMBER 2007 HARDBACK TITLES

ROMANCE

The Italian Billionaire's Ruthless Revenge *Jacqueline Baird*	978 0 263 19716 7
Accidentally Pregnant, Conveniently Wed *Sharon Kendrick*	978 0 263 19717 4
The Sheikh's Chosen Queen *Jane Porter*	978 0 263 19718 1
The Frenchman's Marriage Demand *Chantelle Shaw*	978 0 263 19719 8
The Millionaire's Convenient Bride *Catherine George*	978 0 263 19720 4
Expecting His Love-Child *Carol Marinelli*	978 0 263 19721 1
The Greek Tycoon's Unexpected Wife *Annie West*	978 0 263 19722 8
The Italian's Captive Virgin *India Grey*	978 0 263 19723 5
Her Hand in Marriage *Jessica Steele*	978 0 263 19724 2
The Sheikh's Unsuitable Bride *Liz Fielding*	978 0 263 19725 9
The Bridesmaid's Best Man *Barbara Hannay*	978 0 263 19726 6
A Mother in a Million *Melissa James*	978 0 263 19727 3
The Rancher's Doorstep Baby *Patricia Thayer*	978 0 263 19728 0
Moonlight and Roses *Jackie Braun*	978 0 263 19729 7
Their Miracle Child *Gill Sanderson*	978 0 263 19730 3
Single Dad, Nurse Bride *Lynne Marshall*	978 0 263 19731 0

HISTORICAL

The Vanishing Viscountess *Diane Gaston*	978 0 263 19778 5
A Wicked Liaison *Christine Merrill*	978 0 263 19779 2
Virgin Slave, Barbarian King *Louise Allen*	978 0 263 19780 8

MEDICAL™

The Italian's New-Year Marriage Wish *Sarah Morgan*	978 0 263 19824 9
The Doctor's Longed-For Family *Joanna Neil*	978 0 263 19825 6
Their Special-Care Baby *Fiona McArthur*	978 0 263 19826 3
A Family for the Children's Doctor *Dianne Drake*	978 0 263 19827 0

1007 Gen Std LP

Pure reading pleasure

NOVEMBER 2007 LARGE PRINT TITLES

ROMANCE

Bought: The Greek's Bride *Lucy Monroe*	978 0 263 19495 1
The Spaniard's Blackmailed Bride *Trish Morey*	978 0 263 19496 8
Claiming His Pregnant Wife *Kim Lawrence*	978 0 263 19497 5
Contracted: A Wife for the Bedroom *Carol Marinelli*	978 0 263 19498 2
The Forbidden Brother *Barbara McMahon*	978 0 263 19499 9
The Lazaridis Marriage *Rebecca Winters*	978 0 263 19500 2
Bride of the Emerald Isle *Trish Wylie*	978 0 263 19501 9
Her Outback Knight *Melissa James*	978 0 263 19502 6

HISTORICAL

Dishonour and Desire *Juliet Landon*	978 0 263 19409 8
An Unladylike Offer *Christine Merrill*	978 0 263 19410 4
The Roman's Virgin Mistress *Michelle Styles*	978 0 263 19411 1

MEDICAL™

A Bride for Glenmore *Sarah Morgan*	978 0 263 19371 8
A Marriage Meant To Be *Josie Metcalfe*	978 0 263 19372 5
Dr Constantine's Bride *Jennifer Taylor*	978 0 263 19373 2
His Runaway Nurse *Meredith Webber*	978 0 263 19374 9
The Rescue Doctor's Baby Miracle *Dianne Drake*	978 0 263 19547 7
Emergency at Riverside Hospital *Joanna Neil*	978 0 263 19548 4